Deadline

Hilda Stahl

Cover Illustration by Ed French

bethel publishing
1819 S. Main, Elkhart, IN 46516

DEDICATED WITH LOVE TO
David Woodrow
Who loves a mystery
as much as I do

Chapter 1

She walked to Carla's desk as if she belonged there, the sheaf of typed pages held in her right hand, her left arm swinging free at her side. It was working just as she thought it would. Carla had left the room only seconds before and would be gone long enough for her to leave the story. This really would be a perfect Christmas for her, for Bobby, and, yes, even for Carla Reidel. A shiver ran down her spine. Finally she could put her plan into motion. She had been plotting this since the short story contest had been announced in the August issue of *Woman's Life*. It was a perfect plan, a wonderful, terrible plan. She smiled slightly, savoring the grim secret in her heart. This time it would all work out exactly the way she planned it. This time the right person would die. She would make sure of that. This time she would meet Carla Reidel face to face and shoot her. There would be no chance of someone else dying in Carla's place like the last time. Her fingers curled into the typed pages as she thought of handsome Mark Yonkers. She hadn't meant for him to die. It was really Carla's fault that Mark had died. She should have driven her own car to Thornapple and not borrowed Mark's. He would still be alive today if they hadn't traded for that Christmas weekend. And Carla would be dead. The meticulously planned scheme had backfired, but this time it wouldn't. Her jaw tightened.

Carefully she lifted three sets of paper-clipped stories and laid hers on top of the remaining pile, then dropped the others back in place. No one would notice what she was doing. No one would question her. Perspiration dotted her upper lip and her stomach balled into an icy knot. The fragrance of the long-stemmed red roses next to the pile of manuscripts sickened her and she turned away. Carla wouldn't notice the extra story until this weekend at home when she was reading the others.

She walked away, a slight smile on her face, and only then did she glance around the office at the others busy at their desks. Just as she expected, no one had noticed her going to Carla's desk.

Carla gripped her hairbrush tighter and blinked back stinging tears as she sagged against the bathroom sink. "I must not think about Mark," she whispered brokenly. "I must enjoy this Christmas season!" A tear slipped down her pale cheek. "Oh, Mark!"

Finally she pulled herself up, forced back the agony and carefully touched up her blush and lip gloss, then brushed her smooth shoulder-length sandy hair. Tonight she'd insist that Peter take her home early before he noticed the tired lines around her eyes and started in on her again. He thought she worked too hard, and she knew it was true. But hard work had helped ease the pain of losing Mark. The pain still clung deep inside her, but it wasn't as bad as when he'd first been killed in the car accident two years ago. She bit the inside of her bottom lip and waited for the stab of agony to pass. Would she ever be rid of the anguish? Would she ever stop thinking about Mark? She shook her head. Mark was part of her and she would never forget him. Never! Peter was nice and she liked him, but he wasn't Mark. Impatiently, she pushed the constant struggle to the back of her mind, wrinkled her nose, then sighed tiredly.

This weekend was going to be a real bear. It would take all of her attention and concentration to get through it. She had twenty-five stories to read before she left for her parents' home Monday morning, and out of that twenty-five she had to choose the best one. Greg, Nancy and Peg had already approved of them. Now she would make the final decision.

She should have asked Peter to wait until after Christmas to take her to dinner. She shook her head as she dropped her brush and blush back into her purse. Why put it off? Peter was insistent, and it was becoming harder to turn him down. He had almost convinced her to get on with life, with marriage and a home and family. She hadn't considered such a thing until the past two months. She was sure that Mark would have wanted her to put aside his memory and go on living. It really was easier to *say* than to *do*, especially now during the Christmas season. Every tall blond man made her heart twist. She bit her full bottom lip and leaned weakly against the counter. They would be married by now and have a home in Garden City, maybe even have a baby on the way. But the brakes had failed on her car while he was driving and he'd crashed into the back of a semitrailer. He had lived an hour. She remembered feeling as if she'd died with him, but miraculously she kept on breathing day after day. Finally, Carla moved away from Detroit and her job as assistant fiction editor at *Ladies* to accept a job at Laketown as fiction editor at *Woman's Life*. Little by little she pulled out of her depression and then ten months ago she'd met Peter Scobey. Somehow he inched under her hard shell and became an important part of her life. Like Mark he was editor of a sports magazine, but there the similarity ended. Peter was medium height with dark hair and eyes and was very outgoing. He didn't take no for an answer, nor did he always let her have her own way the way the blond giant Mark had.

Abruptly, she pushed open the restroom door to step into the quiet hallway decorated with a small Christmas tree and red and green streamers along the walls. Her heels sank into the beige carpet and her long skirt swirled around her shapely legs as she slowly walked back to the office.

She stopped in the doorway to find Greg perched on the edge of Madge's desk, talking and laughing, probably trying to get her to have dinner with him. Madge didn't believe in mixing business with her personal life. Jane, typing at high speed, stopped to look up and smiled at Carla. Carla smiled back before she glanced at Kathy, Peg and Lisa, each busy with their own part of the magazine. She walked to her desk, blotting out the quiet talk, usual click of the typewriter keys, and the ever-present sound of rustling pages. In half an hour she'd be on her way to meet Peter for dinner. Then she could go home, soak in a hot tub, dress in her lavender and white sweats, and settle down to read.

She would make this the best fiction edition the magazine ever had. In the time that she'd been with *Woman's Life* circulation had increased because of her work. She smiled, pleased with herself, determined to continue increasing circulation with her powerful stories. She gently touched a delicate red petal of the roses that Peter had sent her, breathed in the fragrance, then sat down on her cushioned chair.

Peg glanced up from the article on nail care that she was editing just as Carla sat down. Now was a good time to catch Carla. Peg's wool skirt split open at the side to reveal a long shapely leg as she walked to the desk. Blond wavy hair framed a classic beautiful face. She waited until Carla dropped her purse in the drawer and looked up. "Carla, did you remember that I need to take off early today to pick up my cousin from the airport?"

Carla frowned, glanced down at her open desk calendar, then nodded. "I had forgotten, but it's written there. When do you have to leave?"

Peg looked at the oak-framed wall clock on the wall above the files. "I think I could wait another half hour if that would help."

Carla sighed and picked up a blue pencil. "Don't worry about it, Peg. Go now if you want and I'll see you back here Wednesday morning."

Peg stepped closer to the desk and leaned down, her blond hair swinging forward. "Did you forget that I'm bringing my cousin to meet you tomorrow afternoon at three?"

Carla closed her eyes for a moment. "I had forgotten, Peg. This is a pretty hectic time for me."

"Would you rather not have us come over?" Peg rested her hands on the desk. She'd promised Amber that she would meet Carla and somehow she'd keep the promise. "We'd understand, but Amber will be very disappointed. She's been looking forward to meeting you ever since I told her we worked together. She's a great fan of yours."

"Then, by all means, come! But I won't be able to visit long."

"That's all right. Amber will understand. She's a businesswoman, too, and she knows how it is to work on a tight schedule." Peg smiled and rested her hands on her narrow waist. "I can't wait to see her. You'll like her. Everyone does." It was still a surprise to her that Amber had called to ask if she could visit a few days, and even a greater surprise that she especially wanted to meet Carla.

"Yes, well, you'd better let me get back to work, or I won't have time for anything but these stories." She rubbed her hand over the pile of manuscripts. "Go meet your cousin and bring her over to my place tomorrow." It was probably a big mistake, but she'd given her word and she wouldn't back out.

Peg's blue eyes sparkled. "Thanks, Carla. See you tomorrow."

Carla nodded, then leaned back as Peg walked away. It might make a nice break in the day tomorrow. Peg was interesting to talk to. Her cousin might be too.

The phone rang and she answered it in a pleasant, but businesslike voice, forcing back her impatience.

"Hi, Carla. I'm glad I caught you before you left."

"Peter!" A tiny spark of happiness flickered inside her, then disappeared. "Is something wrong?"

"I'll say! I can't keep our date tonight. How about tomorrow night?"

She shook her head. "You know I can't, Peter. We'll have to make it Wednesday after I get back from spending Christmas with my folks." This was going to work out after all.

"Wednesday? I can't wait that long, Carla!"

"I'm sorry, Peter. Wednesday or after or not at all." She frowned. Had she really said that to him? Deep in her heart would she be glad if he walked away from her and never looked back?

He was quiet for a long time and she gripped the receiver tighter, wondering if he would tell her to forget the dinner. Actually, she wouldn't blame him if he did.

"Peter?"

"I'm thinking, Carla."

"You know how busy this weekend is going to be for me. We talked about it, remember?" She thought about the wonderful times they'd had together and she bit her full bottom lip. It tasted of lip gloss.

"I can't wait until Wednesday, Carla. I have something to give you before Christmas."

"Sorry."

"You don't sound sorry."

She tapped her toe. "I am very busy, Peter."

"Yes, I can certainly tell." He sounded angry and hurt and she couldn't blame him, but she pressed her lips tightly closed instead of giving in to him. "Goodbye, Carla." He hung up with a bang.

She sighed as she slowly replaced the receiver. She rubbed a velvety rose petal. Peter really was a dear man but at times he pushed her too hard. He wanted more from her than she could give. When she was with him she could almost forget about Mark. No other man had ever pushed Mark out of her thoughts for even a minute.

Just then she looked up to find Jane Varden standing on the other side of her desk. "What is it, Jane?" She tried to keep the impatience out of her voice, but couldn't manage it. Jane should know better than to walk up on her when she was on the phone.

Jane looked down at the floor, her hands clasped in front of her, then lifted stunning blue eyes to Carla. "I just came to tell you to have a nice weekend. I didn't mean to eavesdrop."

"I'm sure you didn't." Carla tucked her hair behind her left ear. "You have a nice weekend, too. Is your husband feeling better?"

"Yes, thanks." Jane smiled, lighting up her plain face. "I'm going to baby him all weekend. As much as he'll let me, that is." She tugged her tan sweater over her dark brown pants. "I'm sorry about, you know, about Peter and your dinner date."

Carla pushed herself up. "Things worked out better anyway. You'd better get going, Jane, or Don will be worrying about you."

"He does worry if I'm late." Jane turned away, then turned back. "Have a nice Christmas."

"You too, Jane." Carla waited until Jane reached the door, then she picked up her briefcase and opened it on her desk. Jane was very hard to get acquainted with, almost as hard as Madge.

Carla glanced across the room at Madge just as Madge looked at her with a scowl. Before Carla could speak, Madge turned on her heel and walked out, her back stiff. Sometimes Madge carried her idea of keeping her personal life to herself a bit far.

Greg walked around his desk, his hat in his hand. "Anything I can do for you before I leave, Carla?"

"Not a thing, Greg. Merry Christmas. See you Wednesday."

He nodded, adjusted his hat on his brown curls and walked out, leaving Kathy and Lisa to say their goodbyes.

"Would you mind if I call you tomorrow or Sunday about a story I'm working on?" asked Lisa as she snapped her briefcase closed.

"Please, not this weekend, Lisa. I've a deadline to meet."

Lisa's shoulders drooped. "I want to be a writer, Carla."

"I know. Keep working at it. I'll see if I can't help you next week. Carla dropped the pile of manuscripts in her case and snapped it closed."

"What would you do if I put another name on the byline and sneaked it in your pile of stories?"

"I'd probably read it. But I wouldn't be very happy about it."

Lisa flushed. "See you Wednesday."

"Wednesday." Carla cleaned off her desk, covered her typewriter and told Kathy goodnight, then walked out with a tired droop to her slender shoulders. Would Christmas season ever get to be an enjoyable, joyful time for her again? Would the memory of Mark's death ever fade?

Tears stung the backs of her green eyes as she walked out into the cold December afternoon, her briefcase in one hand and her car keys in the other.

At the crowded terminal Amber Ainslie walked briskly from the plane into the airport, her blue wool coat slung over one arm and her briefcase in one hand, her purse another. Soft wool pants that matched her coat covered her long shapely legs and touched the black high-heeled dress boots on her feet. A bright yellow cashmere sweater covered a silk blouse of a lighter shade of yellow. Masses of flame-red hair bounced and curled around her slender shoulders and over the back of her collar. Her brilliant blue eyes sparkled and excitement bubbled up inside her as she looked for the tall, sleek blond woman she was to meet. It had been almost two years since she'd spent more than a few hours with her favorite cousin and her conscience twinged as she thought of the way she was using her now. Hopefully, Peg wouldn't question her visit, nor would she discuss the family problems. A band tightened around Amber's heart and she pushed thoughts of her parents aside. Christmas was supposed to be a special time and spending it with Peg might help make it so even if the visit was business and not the vacation that she'd led Peg to believe it was. But was she ready to handle family? Amber nodded slightly as she followed the crowd. She had to be ready. Peg made good cover for her assignment. She peeked around a tall man waring a plaid overcoat and looked over the heads of several women deep in conversation as they walked. Finally she spotted her cousin. To Amber's surprise she was delighted to see Peg. Maybe it had been a terrible mistake to break all family ties because of her parents. She waved the hand that clutched her black leather purse. "Peg! Hi, Peg!"

Peg turned to see the brilliant red-head and with a glad cry, she ran to her and hugged her close, coat, briefcase and all. The fragrant aroma of Amber's perfume delighted her senses. She pulled away, then gripped Amber's arm and led her away from traffic. "Amber, you're really here! How are you? You look absolutely gorgeous."

Amber laughed as she looked Peg up and down. She liked Peg's gold and black plaid coat, matching scarf, and black leather boots. "I could say the same for you." She hugged her again, then stepped back with a smile. "I still can't understand why you're an editor instead of a model."

Peg laughed at the statement that she often heard as she shrugged out of her coat and draped it over her arm. She wore a lilac sweater with several strands of white beads and black wool slacks that she'd changed into before driving to the airport. "I like what I'm doing." She tapped Amber's arm. "And what about you? You could be a high fashion model too with your looks. But you're a tough private detective, one who just happens to own her own agency."

Amber laughed, forcing back a guilty flush. "It's

great, isn't it? And it's great that we're both doing exactly what we want to do with our lives." She fell into step beside Peg and slowly followed the crowd to the luggage area, chattering about her plans. They waited for her matching tan cases to slide down the chute to the circular turntable.

"I'm glad you can spend Christmas with me, Amber." Peg twisted the end of her scarf around her slender hand. "It'll be my first Christmas away from Mom and Dad."

Amber's fingers curled into her purse. Christmastime had been a very special time for her and her family. Would it ever be the same again? She still found happiness in reading and remembering that Jesus had been born to accomplish God's great plan for her salvation, and she'd never let anyone take that from her. But the family togetherness was gone, and that hurt too much to dwell on. She managed a wide smile. "We'll still have fun, Peg." Should she tell Peg that she was here on business and not just to be with her for Christmas?

"Did Aunt Shelia expect you for Christmas?" Peg felt Amber's tension but she recalled her previous promise to herself to have a serious talk with Amber. She had to try to patch up the quarrel between Amber and her parents.

"Mom's going to Hope's."

"Didn't your sister invite you for Christmas?"

Amber took a deep breath and waited to speak until a man and woman in the crowd stopped listening to her and Peg and started talking together. "Hope did invite me, but I couldn't handle going. I don't know if I'll ever be able to. It's something I'll have to work out for myself. Now, I really want to drop this subject, Peg. Please." Tears burned the backs of her eyes, but she refused to let them fall.

"I'll work out the family problems without your help." She saw the hurt look cross Peg's face. "Do you think we can forget everything and enjoy ourselves?"

Peg lifted her chin and bit her bottom lip. "I don't like to see you hurting because of your mom and dad. I want you to make peace with them. For your sake as well as theirs. I got a letter from Uncle Brian just last week and he sounded very upset that you wouldn't write or call. He's your dad and he loves you."

"He doesn't! He couldn't!"

"But he does, Amber."

"Don't!" Amber blinked back scalding tears. All year long she'd pushed away thoughts of Dad and his infidelity, but now with Christmas here, it was almost impossible to forget. It was this time of year that she'd seen him with another woman, that she'd caught him cheating on Mom. It was impossible to forget and enjoy what was supposed to be a joyous season. She took a deep breath and looked Peg right in the eye. "If you continue with this, then I'll take my bags and get on the next flight home. I mean it, Peg. I love you, but I won't listen to anything you have to say about this whole situation." She should have known it would be difficult, but she hadn't expected it to be this hard. If it weren't for her job she would indeed get the next flight home and hole up in her apartment until the New Year.

Peg sighed. "Please stay, Amber. I'll try my best to be quiet about your parents and the divorce and the agony that you're all going through."

A steel band tightened around Amber's heart as the pictures of her dad together with the other woman flashed unbidden through her mind again. Why couldn't she forget it? Dad was human. Was that so hard to understand? Her jaw tightened. No amount of rationalization helped. It had hurt and it still hurt. It was wrong of him to be with another woman when he was married. Adultery was wrong and divorce was wrong. Nothing could change that. The terrible ordeal of the divorce had been almost as hard on her as it had been on her mother. Abruptly Amber pushed the painful thoughts aside and forced her attention to her surroundings. "Look! There's my stuff. It's all there. Isn't that a modern day miracle?" She managed a light laugh as she reached for the bags and lifted them down beside her. Somehow she had to think of today and find pleasure in it.

Peg blinked away sudden tears as she picked up two of the cases, leaving one for Amber. Somehow she had to find a way to ease the pain Amber was still feeling, but what could she do if Amber refused to talk about it? Silently she prayed for wisdom as they walked out of the warm airport into the winter evening. Huge lights shone down on the parked cars and the piles of dirty snow in the parking lot.

In the car Peg turned on the heater, her hands icy. "Do you want to stop somewhere for dinner?" She tried to put warmth in the question, but knew she hadn't succeeded.

Tension tightened Amber's neck muscles as she pulled her coat tighter about her with a shiver. "It's up to you, Peg. I really don't care. Just so it's warm." She forced a laugh as she turned her head to meet Peg's eyes.

Peg smiled. "We could go to Florida."

"We could." Amber grinned and she felt the tension between them slip away. "I had planned to, but I thought about you and decided to see if you would like to spend Christmas with me." The frantic phone call, then the visit from Julie Kadau had actually decided the plans for her. "Cold or not, I'd much rather spend my few days with you than basking in the heat of the Florida sun."

"Sure you would," said Peg with a twinkle in her eye. "We'd both rather stay right here and freeze. We'd better face the truth, Amber. Neither one of us could get enough time off to go anywhere."

Amber shrugged. She could have if Julie hadn't called. "You do have heat at your place, don't you?"

"That I have. And I have a tree waiting for us to decorate together if you want. I have extra groceries. With plenty of vanilla ice cream and fudge sauce." She laughed as she pulled out of the parking space, paid her ticket and drove onto the busy street. Piles of dirty snow lined the street. Car lights stabbed through the gray evening. She glanced at Amber. "You do still eat hot fudge sundaes, don't you?"

"Is Lake Michigan cold?"

"I'm glad I'm not the only one with the family trait. I don't know how you keep your gorgeous figure."

"Same as you, Peg. Exercise and clean living."

"And hard work."

"Yes. Hard work. Lots of it." Dare she tell Peg that she was working now, that she had to find a possible murderer?

Peg lifted a fine brow. "No boyfriend yet?"

Amber thought of Fritz, then forced him to the back of her mind. She'd tried several times to call him before she left, but hadn't been able to reach him. "None. You?"

"None." Peg slowed as a speeding Cadillac passed her, then cut it close in front of her. "But I saw a guy in church Sunday that I thought I'd like to meet. I know he's not married."

"Why didn't you just walk up to him and ask him out?"

"Oh, sure! Can you see that? Besides, by the time I fought my way through the crowd and opened my mouth to do that, Sarah Peterson was already asking him. I slunk away, determined that next time I'd wear tennis shoes instead of high heels so I could run faster and beat Sarah and all the other single gals at church." Peg chuckled as she slowed, then turned left on Patterson Avenue. "In the meantime I've taken up jogging and weight-lifting. It could come in handy the next time."

"You sound as if you never have a date. I happen to know that isn't true."

"Let's face it, Amber. There just aren't that many guys out there."

"That's true. Most people are married at our age." Amber slipped out of her coat, then reached over and turned the heat down a little. She caught a whiff of her perfume, then it was overpowered by Peg's.

"And have a baby or two."

Amber nodded. "But who cares? We're happy with our careers. Aren't we?" Why had she brought it up? Her career was very important to her. It kept her very busy, too busy to think about Mom and Dad or men in general.

Peg sped up to make a green light. "The *I* of we would like a husband and a family. What about the *you* of we?"

Amber sat very still, her hands locked over her leather purse. She would never get married and have it end in divorce. Mom had been strong enough to survive Dad stepping out on her, but Amber knew that she could never endure having the man she loved turn to another woman. "I like my life the way it is, Peg. Honestly. Don't look at me like that. I like being a private investigator. It's a challenge and it pays the bills."

"By the way you're dressed, I'd say it more than pays the bills."

Did Peg know that Grandma had left her a tidy nest egg to make it possible to start her own business? "I'm thinking of taking on another detective. I can't keep up with everything."

"How about me? You could hire me."

"Sorry, Peg. You have the wrong training, but if I ever need a model type, I'll call you." Amber turned slightly in the seat. "Now, tell me about your job. What is it like to work with Carla Reidel?"

"It's really great. She's a genius. We're going to her home tomorrow so you can meet her."

"Super! I can't wait!" Peg must not learn that Carla Reidel was one of the reasons she was here or she might tip her hand to Carla.

"She's working on the fiction contest I told you about." Peg stopped at a red light. "There were several really good stories. She's going to have a hard time picking out one that tops them all."

"Maybe we shouldn't bother her tomorrow. Would it be possible to see her tonight instead?" How casual she sounded! Could Peg hear the wild thump of her heart? Maybe Carla would have the right answers to her questions, and she'd be able to wrap up the case immediately.

The light turned green and Peg drove forward. "Carla's home is on this street. Maybe we should stop tonight and leave her a full day tomorrow to work."

"Sounds great, Peg. But she might resent us dropping in."

"I don't think so. She's nice and we get along fine. She'll tell me if she doesn't want us to visit today. Don't worry about it."

"So you're good friends with her?"

Peg shrugged. "We're friends at work, but we don't visit each other after working hours."

"She's a loner?"

"I couldn't say." Peg shot her a look and Amber knew she had to watch her words carefully.

"Is she married?"

"No, but she goes with a super nice man, Peter Scobey."

"Does she ever talk to you about her life before she moved here to Laketown?"

"No. Why?"

"I just wondered. How about if we stop to eat first, and then visit her?"

Peg nodded. "Good idea. I am starving! How about fish and chips?"

"That's fine with me." Amber watched Peg pull into the restaurant parking lot and park between two Fords. She'd learn as much about Carla Reidel as she could without making Peg suspicious. And she'd keep the conversation away from the family so that they could enjoy each other for the next few days. "I had forgotten what an expert driver you are, Peg."

"Thanks. I enjoy driving." She pulled the key from the ignition and dropped it in her purse, then leaned toward Amber with narrowed blue eyes. "I have always wanted to ask you something, Amber."

Amber tensed. "What?"

Peg laughed. "Relax, Amber. I'm going to stay away from the forbidden territory." She tapped Amber's arm. "Do you ever have a chase scene like the detectives on TV?"

Amber laughed and nodded. "To tell you the truth, Peg, I have."

Peg gasped, her eyes wide. "I want to hear every detail."

"Over fish and chips." Amber opened the car door

and a blast of cold air rushed in. She stood beside the car and pulled on her coat. Somehow she had to learn the truth about Mark Yonkers. Was his death an accident or was it indeed murder as his sister suspected? Maybe Carla had the answer. Amber bent down and looked into the car. "Coming, Peg?"

Peg slipped out her door. "Coming, Amber. And I'm all ears."

Chapter 2

Carla thankfully sipped the hot herb tea that she had discovered in the health food store, then set the cup on the coffee table beside the pile of manuscripts and picked up the top story. The shower had felt wonderful, and now if she could only get her mind off Peter's anger, she'd be able to get on with her work. The brass lamp on the cherry-wood end table cast a soft light over the floral sofa, thick colonial blue carpet and the lavender and white sweats she'd pulled on after the hot shower. Crumbs of a chicken sandwich dotted the delicate bone china saucer beside the half-full teacup. The strains of a favorite piano concerto that she'd played herself once at a concert blotted out the sounds of outdoor traffic. She leaned back with a tired sigh, already scanning the review sheet clipped in place and signed by Greg. She read the story, pulling her pencil from behind her ear to make notes on the review sheet. The story was good, but there was something lacking that she couldn't pinpoint.

The next two stories rated high with her and she saw by Peg's notation that she felt the same. After the third story, Carla stood up, stretched high on her toes with her arms up, rolled her head around on her long slender neck, did four touch-toes, pushed another tape in the player and settled back on the sofa again with her bare feet tucked under her. Working in the privacy of her own small home was much better than working at the office with all the usual interruptions. With an almost totally free weekend she'd finish her project on time.

She glanced at the white phone on the small table near the kitchen door. Would Peter call? She flipped back her hair. She'd hang up on him if he did. He should understand about her work and give her the time she needed. She gripped her pencil tighter. She'd gotten along without him before and she'd get along without him now. Mark's memory had been enough for her up to this point, and it would continue to be so. Hot tears pricked the backs of her eyes, but she blinked them impatiently away.

She snatched up the next story and forced her mind back to her work, then frowned. "Where's the review sheet?" she muttered as she shuffled through the pile, looked around the coffee table and on the floor under the coffee table, but it wasn't there. There was no review sheet. Had Lisa slipped in a story after all? Carla read the title aloud with growing anger. "*Terrible Death* by Susie Archer. Lisa thinks she'll get by with this, does she?" Carla tossed the story aside and picked up the next one. She would not read Lisa's story, not now and maybe not ever! That girl knew better than to do that. And what a title! *Terrible Death* indeed! *Woman's Life* didn't accept that type of story and Lisa knew it very well.

Carla forced aside her anger and impatience and read the next story, making quick notes as she did. The next two stories were quite good and she made notes about them.

Just then the phone rang and Carla let out a tiny shriek and dropped the pages in her hand, then she chuckled softly and shook her head. She was entirely too jumpy. "Let it ring," she muttered, finding her place again in the story. The ringing continued, breaking her concentration, and finally she strode across the room to answer it. Her hand closed over it and she hesitated. If it was Peter what would she say? With her free hand she twisted a strand of sandy hair around her finger. Should she give in and agree to see him? For one brief moment she wanted to have him near, have him hold her close and kiss her until she was weak with longing. She smiled slightly, then frowned and shook her head. She would certainly not give in to him, not now and maybe not ever!

"Hello." Her voice was brisk, and in that one simple word she was able to convey that she was very busy and hated to be disturbed.

"Carla Reidel?"

It wasn't Peter, but a woman speaking in a hushed voice. "Yes."

"Did you read my story yet?"

"Who is this?"

There was a hesitation. "Susie Archer."

Carla pressed her lips tightly together and narrowed her eyes. Lisa! She would certainly learn never to do this again! "I have not read your story and I do not intend to read your story! You know you shouldn't have put it in with the others!" She slammed down the receiver and turned away from the phone to walk to the kitchen for a glass of apple juice.

She sipped the cold juice leaning against the counter near the sink and her treacherous mind flashed right back to Peter. What was he doing and why hadn't he called? Was he with another woman right at this moment?

Jealousy rose up inside her, startling her. Impatiently she plunked her glass on the counter and walked back to her stories.

Susie Archer stared at the pay phone in mute surprise, unaware of the jostling, laughing holiday shoppers or the cars spraying out slush as they drove along the street beside her. How could her plan work if Carla wouldn't read the story? Susie clutched at her throat. Carla had to know what was going to happen to her so that she'd live her last hours in the same pain and agony that Bobby had lived through. He had finally faced the painful truth that Carla didn't love him and never would before he had shot himself in the head with his 12-gauge shotgun. With an unsteady hand Susie clutched the wool scarf around her neck, and took a slow, deep, steadying breath. The plan had to work just right, the deadline had to be met or Bobby's death would not be avenged the way she'd planned, in order for her to live in peace. She had promised to take care of Bobby and make his life happy, but he had killed himself before she could do it. Now that she had found Carla, she would bring Bobby the happiness that he deserved.

Dare she call back? She reached for the black receiver. Perspiration broke out even though the temperature was almost zero. She wouldn't call now. She'd give Carla a little more time to read the story. Right now she would buy the aspirin that had been her excuse to leave the house and then go home. She walked toward the brilliantly lighted drug store, her heart heavy and her head throbbing.

As Peg drove toward Carla Reidel's home, Amber leaned back against the passenger seat and smiled contentedly. She had enjoyed the fish and chips and the lively conversation with Peg. Soon, at Carla's, another piece of the puzzle she was putting together would fit into place.

"I like hearing about your work, Amber. I could've listened all night to the stories about the exciting cases you've solved. You lead a very adventurous life."

"I like it."

"I think I'd get scared."

Amber rubbed her hand over her purse. "I get scared at times, but I do have angels watching over me to protect me."

"That's true. And in your business you need them." Peg grinned and Amber laughed softly. Peg stopped at a red light and glanced at Amber. "When we get to my place we'll decorate the tree."

Amber stiffened. "Sounds like fun."

"I have Christmas dinner planned. Turkey. Not a twenty-pounder like Mom always fixed, but about twelve pounds so that we can have turkey for a week after. And dressing. Cranberry sauce. Should I stop yet?" Peg laughed, then pulled ahead, careful of the traffic.

Amber pressed her hand against her flat, hard stomach. "I am too full to talk about Christmas dinner right now, but please don't leave out the candied sweet potatoes or that special fruit salad that you make so well."

"I'd never forget that. In fact all the ingredients are in my refrigerator right now. Since Christmas is Tuesday I didn't want to wait until the last minute to get groceries. If we go shopping, we want to go for something exciting. Like shoes or clothes or a new ski jacket for me." Peg turned into Carla's driveway and stopped just outside the closed garage door. "This is Carla's place. Nice, isn't it?"

"Small but elegant. I like it. I'm still looking for just the right house for myself." With anticipation

Amber slipped out into the cold night and walked around to join Peg. Soon she'd meet Carla and question her and then maybe she could enjoy the few days with Peg.

Light streamed out of the windows onto the snowy lawn. The sidewalk was swept clean. A Christmas wreath hung on the front door. Peg pushed the doorbell and waited.

"I like the wreath." Amber touched the bright red ribbon and the colored balls on the green boughs. The pleasant smell of pine filled the air. "I was going to hang one on my door at home, but I thought my landlady might take it down and keep it since I'm not there to see. She has this great theory that everything that's mine is hers to use as long as I don't catch her at it."

"Some landlady." Peg frowned at the door and wrapped her coat tighter around her. Maybe she shouldn't have agreed to come tonight instead of tomorrow as planned. "I wonder why Carla isn't answering the door?"

"Maybe she doesn't want visitors." Amber turned to look out at the row of lighted houses up and down the quiet street. Cold wind turned the tip of her nose as red as her hair. She could see her breath as she spoke. "Ring the bell again."

"Maybe we should go home."

"No!" Amber gripped Peg's arm and Peg's eyes widened in surprise. Amber dropped her hand to her side and flushed. "Why should we leave now? We're here and we might as well talk now as later." Amber reached around Peg and held her finger to the doorbell. Peg tried to pull her hand down, but she kept it on the bell.

Suddenly the door burst open and Carla glared out at them, then her face softened. She'd fully expected to see Peter and had been ready to yell at him to leave her alone. "Peg! I thought you said tomorrow."

"We got to thinking that you might want your whole day tomorrow without interruptions, so we came tonight since we were in the neighborhood."

"Come in." Carla stepped aside and Peg and Amber walked into the warm hallway.

"Carla, this is my cousin, Amber. Amber Ainslie, Carla Reidel."

Amber nodded a greeting and smiled warmly. Carla didn't look the elegant lady that she'd pictured, but maybe dressed up she would. "I'm very pleased to meet you."

"Thank you. Please, take off your coats and come in and sit down." She led the way to the front room. "Excuse the mess." Carla motioned to the piles of papers on the coffee table and the floor under the table. "I have several stories to read before I can leave Monday morning for home." She sat back in place on the couch and waited until Peg and her cousin sat in the chairs that flanked the couch.

"I see you've read several stories already," said Peg. "I told Amber about your deadline."

Amber crossed her long legs and folded her hands. Could this woman be a murderer? "I've enjoyed the fiction in your magazine, Carla. You do a marvelous job."

"Thank you. I enjoy it."

Amber listened to Carla talk about her work while Peg carried her part of the conversation. After several minutes Amber said, "Peg told me that you worked on a magazine in Detroit before you came here."

"Yes. But I've been here almost two years and I enjoy the change."

"We have a mutual friend, I believe." Amber watched Carla carefully.

"Oh?"

"Julie Kadau."

Carla stiffened. She didn't know if she could talk about Mark's sister without bursting into tears. "Yes. Julie. I knew her before she was married."

"She lives near me now." Amber glanced at Peg. "Julie said she and Carla were almost sisters."

Carla paled and she fought against the stab of pain.

Amber saw the look of pain in Carla's eyes, but had to continue. "Julie said you were engaged to her brother, Mark, before he died."

Carla crossed her legs and rubbed damp palms down her lavender and white sweats. "It's still very hard for me to talk about it. We were going to be . . . married in February and he was . . . was killed in a car accident in December."

"Oh, dear!" said Peg. She shot a warning look at Amber to get her to drop the subject, but Amber was looking at Carla.

"I'm sorry," said Amber, forcing herself to continue. She uncrossed her long, slender legs, then crossed them again. The glow of the lamp barely dulled the bright yellow of her sweater and the flame-red of her hair. "I didn't mean to bring up a painful subject. It's been two years since he died and I didn't realize it would still hurt so much."

"It does."

Peg moved restlessly.

"At least you still have Mark's family."

Carla tucked her hair behind her ears with a trembling hand. "I don't keep in touch with them. I know I should, but I can't bring myself to do it. I do get a Christmas card from Mr. and Mrs. Yonkers each year."

Amber leaned forward slightly. "Julie knew I would be meeting you and she sent her greetings."

Carla smiled mistily. "I thought she gave up on me. I should have written to her. I almost did several days ago but I didn't have her new address and I didn't want to contact her parents for it."

Amber clicked open her purse. "I can give you her address if you want it."

Carla hesitated. Could she write to Julie without falling apart? Reluctantly she reached for the card that Amber held out to her. "Thanks. I will try to send her a note."

Amber watched Carla drop the address on the coffee table, then settle back on the sofa. "Julie did want me to ask you if you thought Mark's accident was really an accident."

Carla sucked in a great gasp of air and her fine brows shot up almost to her hairline. "What else would it be?"

Amber hesitated, then decided to press on. "Murder."

Carla gasped, her hand pressed to her racing heart, and shook her head. "But how could that be? The brakes failed and he ran into a semitrailer."

Amber leaned forward slightly. "Julie believes that someone, someone who wanted him dead could've tampered with the brakes."

Peg sat very still and listened with wide-eyed amazement.

Even the thought of such a terrible thing sent chills down Carla's spine. "Who would do such a monstrous thing?"

"Julie wondered the same thing."

"But it was my car he was driving and no one knew that we were going to trade cars on that weekend. If anyone had wanted to . . . to kill . . . Mark, they would have done something to the brakes on his car, not mine." Her voice rose and she took a deep breath to steady herself. "The heater on my car was acting up, so Mark said I could drive his car and he'd use mine since he was only driving short distances."

The room seemed to whirl crazily and Amber struggled to bring it back into focus. She felt as if she'd been hit in the stomach. Julie hadn't mentioned that Mark had been driving Carla's car. This shed an entirely different light on everything. She gripped the arms of her chair. "Carla, do you know Susie Archer?"

Carla frowned. Why did that name sound so familiar? "I don't think so."

"How about Bobby Archer?"

Peg looked from one strained face to the other and knew that she wouldn't dare ask for an explanation.

Carla thought about the name, then shook her head. "Should I know them? What do they have to do with Julie and Mark?"

"Susie Archer seems to know you. She mentioned you in a card that she sent to Julie." Amber had promised not to reveal the nature of the message in the card unless it was absolutely necessary. Julie had insisted that Carla not be hurt any more than she already had been.

"That's very strange. But I meet so many people in my business and I read so many names that I couldn't be sure about the ones you mentioned."

What was the connection between Susie Archer and Carla Reidel that Carla didn't know, or wasn't saying? She didn't seem to be lying. "Julie thought it was very strange, too." Actually she'd been terrified, but Amber didn't add that.

"How is Julie? She took Mark's death very hard, too."

"She's fine, I think. Her husband has helped her a lot to face the present instead of looking back on the past. He's a lawyer in Freburg."

"I had forgotten that he was studying law."

Amber relaxed and locked her hands over her knees. "I've worked for him from time to time."

Carla lifted a fine brow. "Are you a lawyer too?"

"Amber's a private investigator," said Peg proudly.

"Is that right? That's very interesting. How did you choose that as a career?" asked Carla.

Amber smiled. "I was always a very curious person and at one time I thought about being a policewoman, then decided to go into private practice. I worked three years with an agency in Grand Rapids, and then I got my own license and my own agency. I enjoy it as I'm sure you enjoy your work."

Carla nodded. "I don't think being an editor is as exciting or as dangerous as being a detective. I'd rather read about life than get out there and face it."

"Me, too," said Peg. "Some of the stories Amber told me were very adventurous and dangerous. Sitting behind a desk is much safer."

"Or sitting here reading these stories," said Carla. "I'd like to ask you girls to stay longer and have a cup of tea with me, but I really must get back to work." She pushed herself up and Amber and Peg stood too. "I've enjoyed the visit, and I do appreciate having the entire day tomorrow to work without interruptions." Hopefully, Peter wouldn't barge in and ruin her day.

"I'm looking forward to reading the special fiction edition, Carla. I hope to see you again when you're not so busy."

Carla nodded. She liked Amber and she did indeed want to get to know her better, but she didn't believe it would happen with Amber living across the state. "Amber, tell Julie hello for me, and tell her to forget the idea of Mark being . . . being murdered." Carla swallowed hard. "I don't think Mark had a single enemy, and I don't want to think that someone actually caused his death."

Amber nodded. "You're probably right, Carla, but Julie did want me to ask your feelings. I think she wants to get on with her life and not have to consider if Mark's death was really an accident."

Carla shivered. "It's too awful to consider!" She walked Amber and Peg to the door and let them out, then stood in the hallway, her mind whirling with the terrible thought that Mark's death might not have been an accident. Finally she walked to the front room to once again bury herself in the stories.

In the car Amber knew she'd have to find Susie Archer as soon as possible and talk to her. Somehow she had to check into Susie's past and see if there was a connection between her and Carla. If Susie Archer was right, Carla was responsible for both Mark's and Bobby's deaths.

Peg drove down the street and turned onto Jefferson. "You're very quiet, Amber."

"Sorry. I was thinking."

"About Carla?"

"Yes."

Peg gripped the steering wheel tighter and kept her gaze straight ahead. "Do you think Mark Yonkers was murdered?"

Amber sighed heavily. "I don't know, Peg, but I do want to find out."

"Why?"

"His sister seems to think he was. I didn't tell Carla, but Julie received a Christmas card from Susie Archer saying that she was sorry about Mark's death two years ago this Christmas, and that Carla had killed him."

Peg shot a startled look at Amber. "Oh, my! Do you think that's possible?"

Amber shrugged and twisted sideways in the seat so she could see Peg's profile. "What do you think? You know Carla better than I do."

Peg stopped at a stop sign and faced Amber. "I don't think she could harm anyone, especially not the man she loved."

"Do you know Susie Archer? She lives here in Laketown."

"I've never heard of her." Peg drove forward and picked up speed, passing lighted homes.

"While I'm here, I'm going to find her."

"You're the detective. It shouldn't be too hard for you." Peg turned into the apartment complex and stopped outside her apartment. "We're home." She slipped out of the car and walked around to the back to unlock the trunk.

Amber joined her while wet, giant snowflakes landed on her hair and shoulders. She lifted out a heavy case and her briefcase, leaving the lighter bags for Peg. "Will you mind if I take time to find Susie Archer?"

"Why should I? Besides, I have this funny feeling that you'd do it even if I did mind." Peg unlocked her apartment door and pushed it open for Amber to enter first. The warm, pine-scented air rushed out at them. A long-needled Christmas tree stood in the corner of the room, looking naked without the usual colored ornaments. A box of colored balls, red and white rope and a string of electric lights sat under the tree on a white tree skirt. On the wall above a crushed velvet gold love seat hung a picture of a graceful ballerina. Beside a green and gold over-

stuffed rocker stood a sound system much like
Amber had in her apartment.

"I like your place, Peg. It's beautiful!"

"Thanks." Peg pushed open the bedroom door
and set the bags on the floor beside a single bed. "I
hope you won't mind sharing the room with me. I
borrowed this bed for you. And I made room for
your things in my closet and dresser." She took
Amber's coat and hung it with hers in the closet.

"This is great, Peg, but are you sure I'm not putting you out?"

"Not at all. This way we can talk all night long if
we want." She thought about the years they were
growing up when they'd had overnights. "Would
you like a cup of tea, or should we get right down to
the serious business and have our hot fudge sundae
now?"

Amber laughed, then shot a look toward the telephone. She had to reach Fritz before he left for the
weekend. "I would like to make a phone call before
the sundae, so how about a cup of tea?"

"I'll get it ready while you make your call."

"Thanks."

After Peg walked out, closing the door after her,
Amber pulled off her leather boots and stood them
neatly at the foot of her bed. She carried the phone
to her bed, sat cross-legged in the middle of it and
dialed Fritz at home. Her stomach tightened and she
was suddenly afraid some woman might answer.
Fritz was divorced and he had many women friends
that she usually ignored. She liked Fritz and knew it
could be more if she'd allow it. They really were
worlds apart when it came right down to it, but there
was something special between them that she
couldn't always ignore.

He answered on the tenth ring and sounded as if

he'd been running.

"Hi, Fritz. Did I catch you at a bad time?" She smiled into the phone as she pictured the tall, broad-shouldered man with thinning brown hair and alert blue eyes racing up the stairs at the sound of his phone. He hated not being able to answer the phone before it stopped ringing.

"Amber! Hey, why are you calling me? You're on vacation."

"I know, but something came up."

"Are you home, Red?"

"No. I tried to call you before I left, but couldn't get you. I'm at my cousin's in Laketown."

"Laketown. I know a man in the police department there."

Amber chuckled. "You always come through for me, Fritz. What's his name and can I trust him and will he help me, or does he have a thing about private cops?"

"So many questions all in one breath! Something is up. Want to fill me in?"

"I will later after I have details. So?" She balanced the phone between her ear and shoulder as she reached for a pad and pencil in her black leather purse. "A name, please, sheriff."

"Les. Les Zimmer. Chief of Police. He's about my age and been on the force as long. He's tough, but he's fair and he has a hard time trusting strangers, especially a woman P.I. A beautiful red-headed brainy type will really throw him."

Amber groaned. "How can I get him to trust me? Shave my head and grow a mustache.?"

Fritz laughed his great bark of a laugh. "That might help."

Amber chuckled, then caught the phone before it fell to her lap. "Aside from that, what can I do?"

"I guess you could toss my name around a bit. That should be good for a few minutes of Les's time." Fritz paused and Amber waited. "But in that few minutes you'd better talk hard and fast and grab his interest because you won't get a second chance."

"I don't know if I'll like this Les Zimmer."

"What's to like? Don't worry about him. He'll help you as long as he knows you're on the level and that you won't keep anything from him."

"Thanks, Fritz." Amber rubbed the soft blue wool of her pants over her knee. "Are you spending Christmas with your son?"

"I'd planned to, but Noreen got this brainstorm to take him to Disney World, so I won't get to. I'm going to be all alone. All alone. Lonely. Sad. Do you feel sorry for me yet?"

"I sure do. You could come here and have Christmas with Peg and me."

"I'll hop the next plane."

"I'll meet you at the airport."

"I'll be wearing a rose behind my left ear in case you forgot what I look like." He laughed again and she laughed with him. "What a nice dream! I'd do it in a minute, Red, but I have to work. Work, work, work."

"And you love it!"

"Yah, I guess I do. About as much as you do, kid. But I'd like to take a vacation now and again, and I think you should too. Let somebody else handle this thing that came up and enjoy your vacation with your cousin. Or better yet, come spend it with me."

"Impossible, my friend." She twisted the white phone cord around her finger. "Fritz, I might have to call you again if I can't get anywhere with your Chief of Police friend."

"You call me anytime, Red."

"I will, and here's Peg's number if you want to call me." She read off the number to him and she could visualize him making a mad scramble for a pencil and paper. "Have a Merry Christmas, Fritz."

"You too, Red. And, Red."

"Yes?"

"Be careful. Hear?"

"I hear. Bye."

"Bye. Red?"

"Yes?"

"Don't fall in love while you're there."

Her heart lurched. "Me?"

He laughed. "I know you're going to wake up one of these days and decide you want a husband and a family, and when you do I want to be there first in line."

"Sure, Fritz. I bet you do. You're always so surrounded with women that you wouldn't notice if I was ready or not."

"I'd notice."

She smiled dreamily. "Merry Christmas."

"Same to you, Red."

"Bye, Fritz."

"Bye, Red."

"Bye." It was a mere whisper and she didn't know if he'd heard or not. She hung up slowly and sighed a long, low sigh as she carried the phone back to the night stand beside Peg's bed. "Fritz, Fritz, Fritz, what am I going to do with you?" Slowly she pushed the pad and pencil back in her purse, then walked out of the bedroom to the kitchen where Peg had placed two teacups and a yellow and white teapot on the small round table.

Peg had clicked in a cassette and the sound of Phil Driscoll's mighty horn filled the apartment. Peg looked over her shoulder at Amber. "Ready for tea?"

Peg closed the refrigerator and walked to the table and sat down.

Amber sat across from her and thankfully sipped the hot tea. "I'll pay for the call, Peg."

"Don't bother."

"No bother at all." She glanced through the open doorway toward the front room. "I think I'm ready to decorate the tree. How about you? I didn't decorate one at home. Carol did one at the office and that seemed enough for me, but after seeing yours in there, I'm all set to trim it."

"Me, too."

Amber followed Peg to the front room where the lamp cast a pleasant glow over the room. A gold drapery over the wide window shut out the outdoors and the music on the stereo system made a pleasant background to work on the tree.

"We'll put the lights on first," said Peg as she carefully lifted them from the box. "I already checked to see that all of them are working. I had to replace a few. I got these from Mom. She said they weren't going to have a tree this year since they were going away, so I got all the decorations that I wanted." Peg carefully hooked the string of lights in place. "Mom wouldn't let me have the special tree-top ornament. Remember it?"

Amber nodded. "A gold star with a dozen or two minuscule colored lights."

"Yes. They bought it on their twenty-fifth wedding anniversary and they don't want anyone to ruin it. That was five years ago."

"I remember." Amber picked up the fluffy white rope and carefully twisted it around the tree, making sure none of the bulbs touched it to scorch it. She didn't want to talk about her happy aunt and uncle or it might lead to discussing her parents. "This is going to be a beautiful tree, Peg."

Peg stood back and admired the tree. "It is, isn't it?"

Amber wound the red rope around the tree and then helped hang colored glass and plastic balls. They finished by draping silver icicles over each branch.

Peg plugged in the lights and Amber turned off the lamp, then they both stepped back and admired the beauty of the tree. "I bought the small angel for the top. It's my very own first Christmas ornament. Isn't she pretty?"

Amber nodded. "Blond hair like yours."

Peg dabbed sudden tears from her eyes. "Amber, this Christmas won't be as bleak as I thought it was going to be. I told my folks that I wouldn't mind missing Christmas with them this year, especially since we had Thanksgiving together, but I was minding it very much. That is until you called. Thanks for coming to share it with me."

Amber stepped forward to adjust a ball so that Peg couldn't see her guilty flush and question her. "It's going to be a good time for me too, Peg."

Chapter 3

Carla absently twisted a strand of sandy hair around her finger as she stared unseeingly across her living room. Why had Julie suddenly started questioning Mark's death? Surely it had been an accident. Anything else would be too terrible to consider. She shuddered just thinking of the possibilities. Suddenly the phone rang, shattering the silence of her living room. She jumped, almost dropping the story in her hands, then frowned.

She was certainly jumpy tonight. It wasn't unusual for her phone to ring this late at night.

She eased up, her legs stiff from sitting with them curled under her, and slowly walked to the phone. Was Peter calling? Her jaw tightened. He'd better not call, not after she told him that she wouldn't have time for him! Since Amber and Peg left, she'd read without a break to make up for lost time, but she knew she'd soon have to go to bed or fall asleep over a story.

The phone rang again and she stood over it, staring down at it. "Peter, are you calling me?" Her pulse quickened, then she frowned as she grabbed the receiver and breathlessly said, "Hello."

"Carla, this is Madge Eckert. Peter and I just had dinner together and we enjoyed each other."

Carla stiffened as surprise was overcome by jealousy. "Why are you telling me this?"

"He doesn't really care about you. And you don't care about him. You're using him and I won't have it!"

Angry sparks shot from her green eyes. "I will not discuss this with you, Madge!"

"Ask Peter about me. I am the special woman in his past that he can't forget."

"He can certainly have you if he wants you!" Carla's voice was shrill with anger. "There is absolutely no reason to call me about this!"

"I want you to stay away from Peter."

"This is ridiculous! How dare you call me and talk to me like this! For a woman who likes to keep her private life to herself, you've certainly brought it all out in the open tonight!" The only answer she received was the loud buzz of the dial tone. She pressed her lips tightly together and slammed down the phone, then locked her icy hands together in front of her. Why should Madge call her about Peter? She didn't care who he had dinner with. Having the night to read had been perfect!

The phone rang again and she scooped it up and barked into it.

"Carla? This is Peter. Is something wrong?"

Her eyes widened and her heart thudded painfully against her rib cage. "I told you that I'd be busy! Why are you calling?"

"I had to find out if you're all right."

"Why wouldn't I be?"

"I was suddenly afraid for you, for us. I must see you!"

"No!" Did he want to tell her that he was going back to Madge?

He was quiet several seconds and she gripped the receiver tighter. "I am going to come over right now, Carla."

"No! I won't let you in!" Why was he doing this? "Then I'll break down the door."

The loud click of his receiver hurt her ear and she jerked the phone away from her head and slammed it back in place. Wouldn't it be better to know the truth? If he wanted to break off with her, then she'd let him so that she could get on with her work. Her breasts rose and fell and her green eyes flashed with anger. How could she face him tonight? It would be better to wait and talk to him on her terms and at the time she chose. She doubled her fists at her sides and nodded. She'd turn off all the lights and go to bed and not answer the door when he came. She shook her head. That wouldn't help. He wouldn't go away until she let him in. She might as well face the fact that he was coming over in a matter of minutes. His apartment was no more than five minutes away. If he broke the speed limit he could be here in two minutes.

With a cry she ran to the bathroom and brushed her hair, covered her lips with a dark pink gloss and brushed blush on her cheeks. Would he notice the dark circles under her eyes? She looked down at her lavender and white sweats and groaned, but there wasn't time to change. She lifted her chin definatly. And why should she change? He was dropping in on her and he'd have to take her the way she was.

The doorbell rang and she clutched her throat and gasped, then ran to the hallway, took a deep steadying breath, and opened the door. Peter walked in, bringing in freezing cold air. He stood only three inches taller than she and was of medium build, but he seemed to fill the hallway. She pressed against the wall as he shrugged out of his dark green leather jacket and hung it in the closet without a word. He wore a dark blue sweat shirt and faded jeans. He gripped her arms and she could smell his after-shave lotion.

"Now, Carla, explain to me exactly what is going on with you."

She tried to pull free, but his grip tightened. "What do you mean? I am working on the stories as you very well know!"

"Why did you call and tell me that you never wanted to see me again?"

"What? When?"

He pushed his face down to hers, nose almost touching nose. "Don't play games with me, Carla. I can't take it the way I'm feeling right now."

"I am not playing games." She saw the pain in his eyes and felt the angry tension in him. "I don't know why you think I am."

He shook her slightly. "Don't you really? You called when you knew I'd be gone and left a message on my answering machine."

"I did not!"

"How can you say that? Should I take you to my place and let you hear the message?"

She shook her head and strained away from him, but still he wouldn't release her. "Peter, stop it! I don't know why you're doing this, but I certainly did not call you. I've been busy most of the night with the stories. If you did get a call from someone pretending to be me, maybe it was your dear, dear friend, Madge Eckert."

"Madge?"

"She called. She said you had dinner."

He nodded. "So what? It was nothing."

Carla's spirit soared. "She thinks differently."

"I don't want to talk about Madge right now. I am going to get to the bottom of this whole deal. You say you didn't call me?"

"I did not call you!"

He grew very quiet, then finally he dropped his hands to his sides and stepped back from her. "You're serious, aren't you?"

"Of course!" She gingerly rubbed her arms where he'd grabbed her.

"Someone called, someone calling herself Carla, and said that she never wanted to see me again, and after Christmas never would. What do you make of that? Why would anyone do that?"

A shiver ran down her spine. "I don't know. It is very strange. Maybe it was Madge." With an unsteady hand she tucked her hair behind her ears. "She warned me to stay away from you. She wants you for herself."

He flushed and shook his head. "She's a silly woman. She knows it's over between us and it's been over for months."

"She could have called pretending to be me just to break us up."

"Maybe so. But it's not going to work." He circled her waist with a strong arm and walked her to the front room and sat with her on the couch. "I broke my date with you tonight because of business, but it turned out that it was only a ploy. Madge conned me into having dinner with her. I tried to be the perfect gentleman and have dinner, but I did tell her that I love you and will always love you."

Carla's heart leaped and she smiled secretly. She did like to hear him say that he loved her, but she wasn't ready for him to know that she liked to hear it.

He leaned back against the couch, his arm possessively around her. "But I wonder what my caller meant when she said that after Christmas I wouldn't see you again?"

"I can't imagine. Monday I'm driving to Thorn-apple to stay until late Tuesday so that I can be with my family for Christmas. Wednesday morning I'll be at work as usual. You know that. Practically every-one I know knows that."

He pulled her tighter to his side. "It must have been a poor joke. Let's forget it." He rested his head against hers. "Since I am here now I want to give you something."

"Oh?" She turned to look into his face.

He swooped down and kissed her. She stiffened but, as the kiss continued, she weakened and kissed him back. Finally he pulled away, smiled softly, then jumped up. "I left it in my jacket pocket. Wait right here while I get it."

She nodded and watched him stride away. With an unsteady hand she touched her lips and smoothed her hair, then folded her hands primly in her lap.

He returned, his excitement tangible, sat beside her and held out a small jeweler's box. "I want you to have this. I didn't want you to go away before I had a chance to give it to you."

Butterflies fluttered in her stomach as she slowly took it and clicked it open. A diamond solitare blinked up at her and she gasped and almost dropped the box.

"Will you marry me, Carla?"

"I . . . I don't know what to . . . say."

"Say yes!"

"I . . . I can't!"

He caught her chin in his hand and turned her to face him. The look in his dark eyes melted her very bones. "I love you. I know that you love me too, but you're letting the memory of a dead man stand between us."

She closed her eyes and whispered, "I know, but I can't seem to help myself."

He lifted the ring from the box and slipped it on her finger. "Wear it home, and give me your answer when you return."

"No, no, I can't! I want to know that you fill my heart before I make such a promise. Right now there is still too much of Mark Yonkers there."

A muscle jumped in Peter's jaw. "It's only an illusion."

Slowly she tugged off the ring. "I must be very sure, Peter."

"At least take the ring and think about it. Please!"

Tears blurred her vision as she pushed the ring back in the box and clicked the tiny box closed. "I can't, Peter."

"Can't? Of course you can!" His voice was harsh. "Forget the dead man, Carla, and get on with your life! I am here and I am alive! Can a dead man hold you and kiss you and make love to you?"

She pushed away from him and scrambled to her feet, her breasts heaving. "You should not have come, Peter! Go away, and stay away!"

He leaped up and strode to the hallway, grabbed his jacket from the hanger and slammed the closet door shut with a bang that rocked a picture on her wall. He reached the front door, then turned and in three steps stood before her. "You will not get rid of me this easily, Carla Reidel. I love you." He caught her to him and before she could struggle, he covered her mouth with his in a kiss that sent her senses reeling. The kiss went on and on and finally she clung to him and returned his kiss with a passion that alarmed her.

Finally he stepped back. "I love you," he whispered. "Your ring is on the coffee table. Do what you want with it." He turned and walked out, closing the door with a gentle click.

She pressed a trembling hand to her thudding heart and stared toward the closed door.

Scalding tears welled up in Susie Archer's eyes and slowly spilled out to slip down her ashen cheeks as she stood at the bedroom window with her fists doubled at her sides. Snowflakes danced in the lights of the houses along the block. In the distance a siren wailed. A light snore came from the bed behind her and she stiffened. She didn't want him to know that she was up and awake again. He worried about her when she couldn't sleep. Lately that had been often.

She shivered from the chill in the room and wished she had slipped on her warm robe. Should she try calling Peter Scobey again? He had to be warned to stay away from Carla before she hurt him like Bobby and Mark Yonkers. Why didn't she hang up when his answering machine clicked on? It had been really dumb to pretend to be Carla. Well, it was too late now. She had left the message and he'd probably get it sometime tonight. Susie shivered again. Too bad she couldn't sleep. It was impossible to get back to sleep once she was awakened, especially when she dreamed about Bobby. The beautiful dream about him tonight had brought her wide awake. He had seemed so alive in her dream. And he would still be alive if it wasn't for Carla Reidel! A muscle jumped in Susie's clenched jaw. Monday Bobby would be revenged. She nodded grimly. Christmas Eve morning she'd go to Carla's house before Carla left for her parents' home and she would shoot her. It would be Bobby's Christmas gift.

Susie bit her bottom lip with white sharp teeth. Carla had to read the story before Monday morning! She had to go through the agony that Bobby had gone through.

Susie tiptoed to the kitchen and picked up the phone and dialed Carla's number before she lost her nerve.

Carla answered on the first ring, sure that it was Peter calling to say goodnight before he went to sleep. He'd left no more than ten minutes ago.

Susie held the receiver rightly to her ear and tried to stop trembling. "Carla, you have to read my story."

"Who is this?"

"You know who it is! Susie Archer. Read my story before you die." Susie hung up, her palms wet with sweat and her heart thudding loudly in the silence.

Carla held the phone away from her and stared at it in sudden fear. "Did she say die?" Carla shivered. Why would Lisa do such a thing? And why call herself Susie Archer? Carla's eyes widened. "Susie Archer! That's why the name sounded familiar to me! Well, she won't get by with this!" Carla flipped open her address book, found Lisa's home number and dialed. The phone rang and rang and rang and Carla's anger rose but fear pricked her skin. Finally she slammed down the receiver and stood back from the phone. This could not go on. Lisa had to be stopped! Amber Ainslie had asked about Susie Archer. Maybe Amber could get to the bottom of this. She was a detective and she'd know what to do. Carla dialed Peg's number and when Peg answered she asked for Amber in an unsteady voice.

"It's for you," said Peg in hushed surprise. "It's Carla and she sounds very upset.

Amber pushed back her hot fudge sundae and took the phone Peg held out to her.

"This is Carla Reidel, Amber. I hate to bother you this late at night, but I have a problem. You asked about Susie Archer. I just learned that her real name is Lisa Dickon, and she used the pen name of Susie Archer." Carla quickly explained about the two phone calls, stressing the fact that Lisa had said she would die. "I tried to call her, but there was no answer. It was frightening to receive such a call even if she didn't mean it literally. I don't have time for this, and I want it stopped. Could you please see what you can do?"

"I'll do my best." Amber gripped the receiver tighter. This was a very unusual turn of events.

"It's a little frightening to get a death threat just because of some story."

"I can understand that. Have you read the story?"

"No! And I refuse to read it."

"Maybe I should come pick it up and read it."

"I don't really think that's necessary. Just do what you can to get Lisa to leave me alone."

"I'll do what I can. But I do want to read the story."

Carla dabbed perspiration off her forehead and upper lip. "I'm going to bed in a few minutes, so if you must read it, stop by late in the morning." She took a deep breath and slowly let it out. "I do appreciate your help."

"I'm glad to do it. We're helping each other, actually. Goodnight." Amber hung up and turned to lick the last of the hot fudge off her spoon, then set her bowl in the sink beside Peg's. "Carla thinks that Lisa Dickon is Susie Archer."

Peg turned from drying the table with a dishtowel. "I know Lisa Dickon and I don't see how she could be Susie Archer. Lisa's from Texas and lived in Texas until last year."

Amber's heart sank. "Are you sure?"

"Very sure."

"Then why does Carla think Lisa is Susie? Carla

has a story that she is sure Lisa wrote and slipped in with the others, and her pen name is Susie Archer."

"I know Lisa is writing a story, but she would never put it in the pile for Carla to read. Lisa knows better."

Amber nodded. "Assuming that you're right and that Lisa is who she claims to be, then there is a Susie Archer out there making trouble. It is very strange that Susie Archer is here in Laketown yet she doesn't have a phone listed in her name, not even an unlisted number. I checked before I left home. Julie doesn't know her and neither does Carla, yet somehow they're all connected." Amber paced the kitchen as she talked. "Is someone lying to me? Is there a connection that someone doesn't want to admit to? If so, why not?"

Peg sank to a kitchen chair and stared up at Amber. "Do you think this Susie Archer means trouble for Carla?"

"I do. If what she said is true, she means to kill Carla. Even though you don't think Lisa is Susie Archer or would want to harm her, I must check her out. Do you have her phone number?"

Peg nodded as she reached for the phone book and flipped to the back. She read off the number while Amber dialed. Lisa's phone rang ten times before Amber reluctantly gave up.

Peg blanched. "This must be a bad dream that I'm having!"

"It's not a dream, Peg. I just wish I knew more details!"

"Why would anyone want Carla dead? Who is this Susie Archer? We must stop her!"

"I know." Amber sat across the table from Peg and folded her hands together on the table and leaned toward Peg. Christmas music played softly in the background. "Who should we talk to first?"

Peg narrowed her blue eyes thoughtfully as she pictured the people she knew were involved with Carla. "How about Peter? Maybe he knows this Susie Archer."

"Can you call him? Would he get suspicious?"

"Not if I said I had a cousin from across the state who wanted to meet him."

Amber laughed. "It would certainly be the truth, wouldn't it?"

"But for a very different reason than what he'd think." Peg reached for the wall phone above the table. "He might be able to help."

"I'll talk to him if he agrees to see us and we'll go from there."

Peg dialed the number and when Peter answered, nervous perspiration popped out on her forehead. "Hi, Peter. It's Peg. Peg Ainslie."

"Peg! I just now walked in the door. What a surprise to hear from you."

"I know. I need a favor from you."

"Oh?"

"My cousin is visiting me from across the state and when I told her I know the editor of *Fish & Hunt* she wanted to meet you. Could we have breakfast in the morning?"

"Does she want me to buy an article?"

Peg bit back a laugh and wished Amber was listening in on the conversation. "No. She's not a writer. She's just very impressed by people who work on magazines. We won't take much of your time. It's important to me. Eight o'clock at Sam's?"

"Sure. Eight o'clock at Sam's. Peg?"

"Yes?"

"I'm not going to have to fight her off with a whip and chair, am I?"

Peg laughed, picturing it. "No. No, Peter. Never that. See you at eight." She started to say goodbye, then said instead, "Did you have a nice dinner with Carla this evening?"

Amber gasped and shook her head, but Peg turned away to listen to Peter's reply.

"No! That Madge Eckert conned me into taking her to dinner."

Peg gripped the receiver tighter and wildly motioned for Amber to come listen. She held the phone so Amber could hear. Blond hair pressed against red curls as Peg continued. "Oh? Didn't you enjoy it?"

"I don't know if you know it, but Madge and I once dated. Madge doesn't want to admit it's over."

"Is that so?" Peg elbowed Amber and Amber elbowed her back. "She's probably angry about Carla then."

"She doesn't have a right to be! Madge and I are finished and she might as well face it." Peter cleared his throat. "You probably are bored by all of this, but you caught me at a bad time. I needed to spill my guts to someone and you called. What better opportunity than to tell all to my good friend, Peg." He chuckled. "I'd better not keep you, Peg. See you and your cousin for breakfast."

"At eight. Peter, I am sorry that your evening with Carla was ruined. Maybe you can make it up to her another day."

"It wasn't exactly ruined. I went to see her a while ago."

Peg nudged Amber again. "How's she coming with the stories?"

"She's sure she'll meet her deadline."

"That's good."

"See you in the morning. And your cousin."

"See you. Sleep well tonight. Bye, Peter." Peg

hung up and turned to Amber with sparkling blue eyes. "We'll talk to him in the morning. Maybe he will be able to help. Can you believe that Madge Eckert? She works in the office and she won't have anything to do with any of us. So—she had dinner with Peter. I wonder what Carla thinks of that?"

"How well do you know this Madge Eckert?"

"Not very well at all."

"How long has she lived here?"

Peg shrugged. "That I couldn't say. Peter should know. You can ask him tomorrow."

Amber tapped Peg's arm as they walked to the bedroom. "You handled the talk with Peter very well. I think I'll be able to use your help. Detective Peg Ainslie. It has a nice ring." They laughed together as they got ready for bed.

Saturday morning, after trying unsuccessfully to reach Lisa again, Amber stopped just inside the doorway of Sam's to watch Peg step forward to hug Peter and receive his kiss on her flushed cheek. He had dark hair and eyes, an average build, a tiny scar at the left corner of his wide mouth and was probably in his late twenties or early thirties. He was easily one of the best looking men she'd ever seen. Peter was dressed in dark pants with a blue and gray pullover shirt and a tan leather jacket. His voice was pleasantly masculine as he asked Peg how she was.

"I'm fine, Peter, and glad that Christmas is almost here." Peg turned toward Amber. "My cousin and I are going to have an enjoyable Christmas together. Amber Ainslie, Peter Scobey."

"Hello, Peter." Smiling, Amber held out her hand and Peter clasped it warmly while his eyes said he liked what he saw. She knew he was getting the same message from her and she didn't try to hide it. Long ago she learned to trust the knowing feeling inside her. That same feeling was telling her that she could trust Peter Scobey completely.

"I'm glad to meet you, Amber." He released her hand and motioned for her to precede him. "I hope you enjoy your vacation."

"I'm sure I shall." Amber sat at the small square table with Peg at her right and Peter at her left. The restaurant was almost empty. Music played in the background and waitresses tried to occupy their time while waiting for people to walk in. Sounds of muted voices and clattering dishes and silverware came from the kitchen. At the long counter two people sat eating French toast and drinking coffee.

"Peg tells me you're not a writer, Amber. What do you do?"

"I have my own business in Freburg." She smiled easily and quickly changed the subject. "It must be very exciting to edit a sports magazine, Peter. Have you worked there long?"

"Almost ten years. Right out of college."

Peg moved restlessly, wondering if she should keep quiet or bring up Carla's name. "Our dads subscribed to your magazine. Didn't they, Amber?"

Amber's jaw tightened and she nodded stiffly. Peg knew she shouldn't have brought up Amber's dad. "Where'd you attend college, Peter?"

"U of M. How about you?"

"Grand Rapids." Amber turned quickly to Peg. "And you attended a school in Detroit, didn't you?"

Peg nodded, and launched a discussion about her college days, working easily into Peter talking about his past without making it too obvious.

After an omelet with cheese and bacon along with coffee and orange juice Amber said, "You're the second editor I met since I arrived yesterday, Peter. Last night Peg and I dropped in on Carla Reidel. I was pleased to meet her."

"She's a wonderful person," said Peter. "It's no secret that I love her."

Amber and Peg exchanged knowing looks, then Amber said, "Does that mean wedding plans for the two of you?"

Peter shrugged. "Maybe. I'm hoping so."

"I'd like to be invited to the wedding," said Peg.

"Count yourself invited." Peter grinned. "If I can convince Carla to forget the man from her past."

Amber jumped on that like an Ainslie on a hot fudge sundae with nuts. "Mark Yonkers? The man killed in the car accident?"

Peter nodded. "Did she tell you about him?"

"Yes. I know his sister Julie. Have you ever met Julie or any of the others in Mark's family?"

Peg locked her hands in her lap and bit the inside of her bottom lip. Did Amber know what she was doing?

Peter leaned forward with a frown. "I haven't met anyone from Carla's past. I do know how hard she took Mark's death, and how hard it still is on her."

Amber finished the last of her coffee, but refused more when the waitress offered another cup. Peg and Peter accepted another cup of steaming coffee before the waitress walked back to the counter. Amber crossed her legs and rubbed her hand over the knee of her dark pants. "Peter, Carla seems to be in danger and she needs help. I've offered to help her. Peg and I think that you will want to help also."

The color drained from Peter's face. "Danger? From what? Who? What kind of help does she need?"

Peg caught Peter's cold hand between both of hers and held it tightly, thankful that Amber had decided to trust Peter. "Try not to worry. Amber is good at her job."

Peter turned to Amber and his dark brows shot up questioningly.

"I'm a private investigator, Peter. I am looking into Carla's past to see who would want to harm her. If you know of anyone, please tell me."

"Who would want to hurt Carla? She's a wonderful woman. I can't believe she has a single enemy. Wait a minute! I got a phone call last night that frightened me. A woman called saying she was Carla." Peter's voice cracked and he took a deep breath to steady himself before he finished his story. "I will do anything I can to help."

"How long have you known her?"

"I met her when she first came here almost two years ago, but I didn't get to know her until about ten months ago. We've been going out together and during the past two months we've gotten quite close." He looked helplessly from Peg to Amber. "Can't we go to Carla and stay with her to keep her out of danger? What kind of danger do you mean?"

Amber kept her voice low to keep the passing waitress from overhearing her. "Physical danger, Peter."

This morning while they were dressing Amber had told her that she had to proceed with the investigation with the assumption that Carla was in real danger.

"Someone has threatened to kill her," whispered Peg through stiff lips.

"What?" Heads turned and Peter flushed and lowered his voice. "What are you saying? That's impossible! This is not the movies."

Amber nodded sympathetically, then quickly told him as much as she could. "Murder happens in real life whether we like it or not. But I am going to do all I can to protect Carla and to stop the person trying to kill her." She lowered her voice even more. "Peter, does the name Susie Archer mean anything to you?"

"No. Should it?"

"She threatened Carla."

"Then find her and put a stop to this whole thing!"

"That's just what I plan to do. But if she doesn't want to be found, then that makes my job a little harder. After I leave here I'm going to meet with the Chief of Police while Peg goes to the library to do a little research."

"I'll check into the accident in back issues of newspapers," said Peg.

Peter's jaw tightened. "I am going to Carla's and I'm going to stay with her until you get this dealt with." He shook off Peg's hand and pushed back his chair.

"Sit down and listen then." Amber waited and knew by the look on Peter's face that he couldn't decide whether to go or stay. Finally he dropped back to his chair and faced her with a grim look. "Peg tells me that you know Madge Eckert."

He nodded slightly, his jaw set. "What about her?"

"I need to know how long you've known her and how long she's lived here."

Peter frowned thoughtfully. "I don't know how long she's lived here. I've known her a year I'd say. I broke up with her a few months ago."

"Would she want to harm Carla?"

"I know she is jealous of her, but I don't think she would actually harm her. Not Madge. I don't think so, anyway. She was very angry when I wouldn't go back to her and drop Carla. She did call Carla and warn her to stay away from me. Maybe she did the rest." He slammed a fist into his palm. "If it was her, she won't get by with trying to hurt Carla!"

"Maybe it wasn't Madge who made both calls, Peter," said Peg. "Amber thinks it could be someone else, someone who knew Carla years ago, someone trying to taunt her with even more than just the story."

"So, Peter, don't accuse Madge of making the call." Amber dropped her wadded paper napkin onto her empty plate. "We can't rule out the possibility that Madge is behind the murder threat."

"Oh, I don't think she'd go that far." Peter shook his dark head. "I don't think she would."

"I want to check it out so don't do anything to tip her off. It is entirely possible that Madge is Susie Archer. Now, let's all get going. I don't know how Carla will take it if you try to stay with her." Amber picked up the check that the waitress had dropped between her and Peter. "Tell her that we discussed the events with you and hopefully that will give her the freedom to talk to you about it. If she tells you anything that you feel we should know, call us at Peg's apartment."

Peter nodded and strode away, his shoulders square and his head high.

"He's upset," said Peg.

"I know." Amber sighed heavily. It was hard to see people in pain, but it was part of her business. "I'm going to stop at Carla's and pick up that story after my appointment with the Chief of Police."

Peg pushed her empty water glass away from the tip that she'd dropped on the table. "Maybe I'll know who wrote it after I read it. At least I'll know if a professional writer wrote it. Is it possible that this whole Susie Archer deal is a coincidence? Maybe someone picked that name out of a hat to hook to the story. Maybe it has nothing to do with the Susie Archer who sent a note to Julie."

"That is possible, not very probable, but indeed possible." She'd seen stranger things happen. She pushed the chair up to the table and walked toward the cash register.

With a steady, determined hand Susie Archer slowly, methodically rubbed the oiled cloth over the long barrel and smooth stock of Bobby's 12-gauge. A dull pain throbbed in the back of her head and she bit her bottom lip to hold back a moan. Once all of this was over she'd be able to get a good night's sleep.

"Are you cleaning that gun again, honey?"

She looked up, flushed with guilt, and nodded slowly. Her nerves tightened, turning the dull pain in the back of her head to pounding agony for fear he might learn what she was going to do. He'd try to stop her if he even suspected. He might even stop loving her, and that she couldn't endure. He was a nice man, too nice at times. It was totally against his nature to take revenge. He wouldn't understand her need at all. At times she didn't either. With a trembling hand she rubbed the shotgun barrel one last swipe. "It's the only thing left of my little brother's."

Gently he took it from her and hung it back on the brackets above the closet door. "He's been dead a long time, sweetheart."

She hung her head. "I know."

"Long before we met and fell in love. Since Christmas six years ago. It's time to forget it and get on with your life."

Her head snapped up. "Christmas Eve morning six years ago."

He rubbed his hands gently up and down her arms and looked deep into her eyes. "Christmas. Christmas Eve morning. What does it matter now?"

She shrugged and lowered her eyes so he wouldn't see the anger and hatred. It did matter. It mattered a lot. Especially to Carla Reidel.

"Let's have breakfast, honey. Okay?"

She forced a smile as she slipped an arm around him and walked toward the tiny kitchen. Food stuck in her throat, but so far she'd kept it from him. "Eggs and bacon?"

He sat her on the stool at the counter and placed a long, lingering kiss on her dry lips. "You sit here and watch and I'll cook this morning. You look a little tired again this morning and I don't want you getting sick at this special Christmas time."

Tears stung her eyes as a fiery, possessive, all consuming love for him rose up inside her. She clung to him so tightly her arms ached. In all her life he was the only person who had ever loved her, aside from Bobby. He kissed her again, then eased away from her. "Orange juice, too?" She nodded, unable to speak around the hard lump in her throat.

Chapter 4

Cold wind blew against Peter's back as he ran to Carla's door and frantically pressed the bell. In the Saturday morning stillness he could hear it inside ringing on and on and on. Sweat broke out in his armpits and he doubled his fist and pounded on the door. The cold wind whipped a scrap of newspaper across the lawn and it caught against a barren shrub near the sidewalk. A car drove past, followed by two others. A boy on a bicycle whistled Jingle Bells, then pedaled out of earshot. Peter jabbed the doorbell again, leaving his finger on it longer still. Was she asleep? Or maybe in the shower? Why didn't she answer? A muscle jumped in his taut jaw. Maybe she'd seen him on her step and wouldn't answer. His stomach tightened and he growled low in his throat.

He glanced toward the garage and a strange feeling filled him. He ran to the garage and peered through the small glass on the side door. The garage was empty. Carla had gone somewhere. But where? Had someone called her away from home to kill her? He groaned and ran to his car, the cold nipping at his ears and fingers. Maybe he could find her. He slipped into his warm car and gripped the steering wheel until his knuckles turned white. His eyes darkened with fear. Who was he kidding? There was no way that he could drive up and down each street until he spotted her car. He drummed the steering wheel impatiently as he stared unseeingly at her garage. He couldn't just sit here and wait or he'd go crazy.

"Madge! I'll go talk to Madge and see just how far she'll go to keep Carla and me apart!"

Inside the house Carla watched Peter speed away. For one wild minute she wanted to run after him and shout for him to come back. Instead she lifted her chin defiantly and slowly turned away from the window. Her plan had worked. She pushed her hands into the pockets of her jeans and nodded. She'd asked the neighbor if she could park her car in his garage while he was gone so that when anyone, especially determined Peter, came to the door to bother her, they'd see that her car was gone and assume that she was too. Her neighbor would be back in about three hours, and then she'd drive her car into her own garage. She grinned. It really was quite an ingenious plan.

"Now, I can get back to work," she muttered. She walked to the couch and sat down to read another story. Against her will and her better judgment she picked up Lisa's story and looked at it again. "Susie Archer indeed! Lisa will certainly not get by with this!" She dropped the pages on the coffee table and sat on the couch, her eyes never leaving the story. Why on earth would Lisa tell her to read it or she'd die?

"What a waste of my time!" Carla leaned forward to pick up the story, then frowned at the sight of her name on the first line. "Very funny." Lisa didn't go in for practical jokes, and everyone knew that. Someone was playing a trick on her. If it wasn't Lisa, then who? Greg? He liked to tease her. But would he do this?

He knew her tight deadline. Besides, he'd never ask a woman to call her and threaten her. She should toss the story aside and forget it. But for some strange reason she couldn't put it aside. A shiver ran down her spine and she gripped the pages tighter. With an impatient sigh she sank back and read.

Bobby Archer loved Carla Reidel. Carla Reidel loved Bobby Archer. I know they loved each other very much. I watched them together and I could tell by watching them talk and hold hands and kiss that they were in love. I listened to Bobby talk about Carla night and day. I was his sister, the only family he had, and he talked to me a lot. He wanted to marry her. He was sure she wanted to marry him. She was a junior in high school and he was a senior. He was so sure that they'd get married that he designed a wedding invitation special for them.

Carla moistened her suddenly dry lips. "Bobby Archer! I remember! And his sister Susie!" What was going on here? Who knew about her past to write about it? Or had Susie herself written it? Carla bit her bottom lip. She hadn't talked about, or even thought about, Bobby Archer for years. She'd barely known Susie. Carla shook her head impatiently. She hadn't talked to anyone in Laketown about her high school days. Had she? Surely she wouldn't have mentioned the few months that she'd been desperately in love with odd Bobby Archer. She had loved him because he was the underdog. When she realized that was the only reason she loved him, she'd dropped him. She tugged at her neckline and rubbed a damp palm down her leg. "I certainly will not waste my time reading this!" She flung the clipped pages to the coffee table, then scooped them up before they had a chance to settle in place, and continued to read.

I tried to warn Bobby not to get involved with Carla. She had rich parents and we lived in a foster home. We'd always lived in foster homes, but not always together. Nobody loved us and that's why Carla was so important to Bobby. It hurt me to see her use him, but he wouldn't listen to anything bad I said about her. I made up my mind to take Bobby and leave the foster home. When I had a chance to get out on my own I took it and I promised Bobby that he could come live with me the minute he was eighteen and out of high school.

There wasn't a chance for that. Bobby finally realized that Carla didn't love him and that she'd never marry him. Bobby shot himself.

Carla gasped, her hand trembling against her parted lips. Now it was all coming back to her! Bobby had shot himself, but she thought he'd done it because he hated his foster parents. Had he really shot himself because she had broken up with him? It couldn't be! Surely he hadn't loved her that much. His sister had probably needed someone to blame and had picked her. But why the story? And why now after all these years? How in the world had the story been put on her desk? She shivered and shot a look around her peaceful room to see if someone had invaded her home as well as her office. She took a deep breath to steady herself, skimmed a couple of pages that told how devastated Susie had felt about her brother's death and how angry she was at the girl responsible for it. Susie told of her mental breakdown and the time she had spent in the state hospital where the doctors had worked with her to get her back to normal.

I swore that I'd get even with Carla Reidel if it was the last thing I did. I never let Doctor Everett know how I felt or he might've thought I shouldn't leave there. I told him that I knew Bobby was the only one responsible for his death. He believed me. So did the nurses that acted like they felt sorry for me or something. I didn't need their pity!

After I was released from that terrible institution I searched for Carla, but she'd moved away. Finally, after a long search I learned that she was editor of a magazine in Detroit. I found her. She didn't know it. I was very clever. I planned a way to kill her. But her fiance died instead. I fixed the brakes on her car and the car crashed into the back of a truck. But Carla didn't die. Mark Yonkers did.

"What! What?" Carla's voice rose to a shriek and the papers fell from her lifeless fingers. The color drained from her face, leaving a sickly gray pallor. She cradled her arms against her chest and whimpered like a frightened, hurt child. This had to be a nightmare! She stabbed trembling fingers through her sandy blond hair.

Was it possible that Susie had killed Mark? Carla looked down at the scattered pages and mutely nodded. His death had been no accident if she could believe what she'd just read. Julie had been right to be suspicious. Mark had been deliberately murdered. She was without the man she loved because of some crazy person!

She shook her head hard. "No, no, no. This isn't happening." She rubbed her hands over her jeans, touched the cold teacup, picked up the saucer that had held a piece of toast with strawberry jam, and set it back in place. She was awake. It was morning, Saturday morning. It was not a nightmare. Susie blamed her for Bobby's death and had tried to kill her two years ago. Mark had died instead. The police had investigated the accident and there had been a question about the brakes, but then nothing had come of it. The police had called it an accident. She had called it an accident, and so had Mark's family. Now, suddenly Susie Archer, or someone writing as Susie Archer, stated that it had not been an accident, but had been deliberately planned. Could it be the truth? Scalding tears filled her eyes and she impatiently brushed them away. This was not the time to dissolve into wild tears. She had to stay calm and decide what to do. Tension mounted and her brain whirled.

She ran to the phone and with trembling fingers called Peg's number. Amber had to know what she'd just learned! Amber would know what to do; it was her business to know. The phone rang until Carla lost count and finally in despair she hung up.

"Peter! I'll call Peter!" He'd had plenty of time to get home. She dialed his number, her breathing ragged. He answered and she cried out to him, only to realize it was his answering machine. She dropped the receiver in place with a loud clatter without leaving a message.

Who else could she call? The police? She frowned and shook her head. She'd talk to Amber first before she did anything that desperate.

With a shudder she walked back to the couch, sat down and reached for the scattered pages. Putting them in order with shaking, icy hands, Carla found where she'd left off. The words blurred, then finally focused so that she could continue to read.

I hid away from everyone after that, afraid that I'd be found out, but Mark Yonkers' death was called an accident. I was sorry that he had died, and it still bothers me to think about it. It really was Carla's fault. She should have used her own car to drive to Thornapple that weekend, and she would have died. I tried to tell Mark Yonkers' family that it was Carla's fault, but I don't know if they believed me.

I lost track of Carla for a while after that and I was frantic. But one day I read that she was fiction editor of Woman's Life, *so I hunted until I found her. I know where she works and I know where she lives. I've watched her every day for months. I work beside her and she doesn't notice. I talk to her, but she doesn't recognize me with my new color of hair and contact lenses and more money to dress myself properly. Now, I am going to kill her. I am going to use the same shotgun on her that Bobby used on himself. There won't be any way for me to kill the wrong person this time. I will aim the shotgun and fire and I will kill Carla Reidel. Bobby will be revenged and I will, at long last, live in peace.*

Carla, this could be the very last story you will ever edit.

Cold sweat broke over Carla's body and she jumped up, dropping the story as if it burned her fingers. She backed away from it and stared down at it scattered on the blue carpet. Her stomach knotted into a hard, icy ball. Did Susie really mean to kill her? Was this honestly happening to her? Maybe she'd worked so hard the past two years that she'd finally had a mental breakdown.

She dropped to her knees on the carpet and frantically pulled the papers to her and scanned the pages again. Yes, the words were there. Susie Archer meant to kill her. Unless this was a horrible practical joke someone was playing on her. She shook her head and groaned. "No, no, this is no joke." She did indeed have something to fear. Should she call the police? Would they take the story seriously, or would they think it was only fiction? For a long time she sat on the floor staring at the story in her hands while Christmas music played on the radio in the background.

The phone rang and she shrieked and fell back, then scrambled to answer it. She said hello and her voice cracked and hurt her throat.

"Carla Reidel?"

The whispered sound sent a chill down her spine. "Yes."

"Have you read my story yet?"

Carla gripped the receiver tighter and shivered. "Who . . . who is this?"

"Susie Archer, of course. Did you read my story?"

"Yes!"

"I am going to kill you."

"No!" Carla sagged against the wall, the phone pushed against her ear. "Is this a joke?" She forced out the hoarse whisper around the painful lump in her throat.

"This is not a joke, Carla. I am going to shoot you. But first I wanted to give you time to suffer just as Bobby suffered when you broke his heart."

"I'll call the police!" She meant for the words to come out forcefully, but instead they were a weak whimper.

"They won't believe you."

The perspiration on her hand made the phone slippery. "Stop it! Don't do this!" Her voice broke and her mouth felt cotton dry.

"You hurt Bobby." The voice rose. "You made him shoot himself. You have to die!"

Frantically she shook her head. "It wasn't my fault! I didn't mean to hurt him!" The receiver clicked and she heard the buzz of the dial tone. "Don't you do this to me!" She screamed into the receiver, her fingers tight around it. The neutral buzz answered her. With a cry she slammed the receiver in place and stared down at the phone on the low table. It swam before her eyes and she blinked fast.

The thud of her heartbeat drummed in her ears. Cold sweat soaked her body. Trembling uncontrollably she sank to the floor and leaned her head against the low table, too weak to dial the number for the police. "Peter. Peter, I need you. I need you," she whispered hoarsely as tears streamed down her ashen cheeks and wave after wave of fear crashed over her.

Numbly Susie Archer dropped coins in the pay phone, dialed the police and when a woman answered, she said in a clear, firm voice, "This is Carla Reidel calling. I'm the fiction editor of *Woman's Life* and I live at 612 Greenwood. I don't quite know how to say this, so I'll just say it. In just a few minutes a woman will be calling you to tell you a wild story about murder and a threat on her life. She will say she is Carla Reidel, but it will be a practical joke. She has read one of the stories I have for my magazine and she is trying to make it appear true. I tried to stop her, but she is determined to call just to see what you will do. I know she shouldn't make a call to the police for a practical joke and I tried to talk her out of it, but she wouldn't listen to me. She is studying theater and she said that she could easily convince the police that her story is true. I'll try again to talk her out of making the call, but I don't think that I can. I don't want her to get into serious trouble so disregard the call, please."

She hung up, smiled a slow, secret smile, then walked to her car to drive home. Carla was indeed suffering. Taking the chance that Carla would recognize her voice by making so many calls had been worth it.

At the police station Amber walked briskly to the glass door marked Chief of Police. Hopefully the visit to Les Zimmer would be productive. He was expecting her only because she'd dropped Fritz Javor's name during the phone conversation. That had worked remarkably well. She glanced over her shoulder at the large room filled with desks, some occupied and some empty since it was a Saturday. Two men looked her up and down, then dropped their eyes when they saw she was looking at them. Cigar smoke hung in the air and she wrinkled her nose and tried not to breathe. Telephones jangled noisily, and were answered in voices too low for her to hear any of the words as she knocked.

"Come in." It was a bark more than an invitation.

Amber clutched her black leather purse tighter, made sure her purple silk blouse was tucked neatly into her black slacks, then opened the door and sailed in with a wide smile and a cheerful greeting. The high heels of her black leather boots clicked loudly on the floor.

Les Zimmer looked up, then scowled. He was a slight, wiry man dressed in a navy blue sweat shirt that had years of wear and faded jeans that hugged his narrow hips and thin legs. "What d' ya want, lady? I have an appointment with a private eye and don't have time for you."

She was used to that and she smiled and stopped just inches from his desk. "I'm Amber Ainslie and I have the appointment with you."

He blinked and that was the only look of surprise he allowed to show. Without standing, he waved her to a chair. "Sit down and tell me what's so important that it couldn't wait until Monday."

She sat down, crossed her long legs and tucked her purse in between her thigh and the arm of the chair. As quickly and concisely as she could she told him that she was looking for Susie Archer and that Susie Archer had threatened Carla Reidel. She did not tell him that her instinct told her to believe Carla was in immediate danger. Les Zimmer would never go for that. "I thought you could help me find Susie Archer."

"Why wasn't I informed that a threat was made against this Carla Reidel?"

"She doesn't take it seriously."

He lifted a dark brow. "Oh, and you do?"

"I have to look into it."

"But you can't find this Susie Archer?"

She saw the smirk on his face and sparks flew from her sapphire blue eyes before she could mask her anger. "No, I can't."

"You need my help? Is that it?" With a dry chuckle he nodded in response to his own question as he reached for the ringing phone and answered it gruffly. He talked a few minutes while she patiently waited, then slammed down the black receiver. He jumped up as if he couldn't bear to sit still a second longer and walked around the desk. He wore high top black and white running shoes with the laces hanging down to click on the floor. "Just what is it you want from me?" He lifted a foot to an empty oak chair and tugged his laces snug and tied them, then dropped that foot and did the same to the other. "You want me to do your investigating for you, then sit back and watch you get paid for my work?"

Amber took a deep steadying breath. She would not allow him to get to her! "I need to know if you have anything on Susie Archer."

He walked to the coat tree, touched his denim jacket, then turned around to face her. "I guess it won't kill me to get that for you."

"Thank you." She kept her voice very business-like.

He picked up his phone and barked into it while she listened, hiding a smile. Fritz had been correct about Les Zimmer.

A uniformed officer stopped outside the glass door, raised his hand to knock, then walked away when he saw Amber.

Les walked across the room, a thumb looped in

his back pocket. He didn't speak and she didn't either. After a while the phone rang again, breaking in on the silence. He turned away from her to answer, talked a while, hung up and turned back to her. "We don't have anything on Susie Archer. Neither does D & V."

"Yet she lives here in town. Probably under an assumed name."

"Assuming she's not part of the fiction at that magazine."

Slowly she stood and looked him squarely in the eye. "She is not fiction, Les."

He shrugged. "If you say so."

"I say so." She lifted her chin a fraction. "I'd like access to your computer to see if Bobby Archer existed and, if he did exist, find out when he died.

Les held up a hand, palm out. "Hold your horses, Red."

She stiffened and lowered her eyes momentarily to hide the flame that leaped out. No one except Fritz dared to call her Red. She decided to let it go. She needed a favor.

"You don't touch our computer." He stopped before her and stood eye to eye with her, almost nose to nose. She didn't budge an inch. Without the high heels on her boots she would have been shorter, but, as it was, she stood the same height. Fritz Javor towered over her and from what Fritz had said about Les, she'd expected him to be a giant of a man also. Finally Les stepped back from her and she saw a twinkle in his eye. "You go right ahead and use the computer, Red. We'll see if you're wasting my time."

She smiled ever so sweetly. "But it wouldn't be a waste of time for me. Now I can tell Fritz that I got to meet you."

"Yah, real big deal." He stood with his hands

resting lightly on his thin hips, his feet apart, and grinned.

"Fritz said it would be." She chuckled softly. She wouldn't tell him what else Fritz had said.

Les turned as a uniformed policewoman walked in with a foldout sheet. He took it from her with a gruff thank-you and she walked back out without more than a quick glance at Amber. Les spread the sheet on the desk and bent over it. "I've been waiting for this. Won't be a minute." She could smell an earthy soap smell on his dark skin. Finally he turned back to her. "You still here?"

Amber nodded. "How about the computer?"

"Do you know how to use a computer?"

Did she look stupid to him? "I have one in my office in Freburg."

"Freburg, you say. I thought you were from Bradsville."

"It's nearby. My home is between the two places."

"I see." He walked to the glass door and threw it open. "Help yourself to the computer over there. Just show me what you get."

She nodded and smiled. "Thanks, Chief."

"Save the thanks for later, Red."

She bit back a sharp retort and walked to the computer.

Several minutes later she had the information of Bobby Archer's death in her hand and she walked to Les's door and knocked. This time when he barked for her to enter, she laughed under her breath and walked in.

"Here it is, Chief. Bobby Archer died six years ago in Thornapple of a self-inflicted gunshot wound to the head." The note Julie had received was totally wrong. Carla had not been responsible for Bobby's death.

Les grabbed the information from her and read it.

"From this you're thinking Susie Archer is out there on the loose trying to kill off Carla Reidel? You don't have much to go on, Red."

She grabbed back the report. "I have to use what I have!"

He rubbed his jaw and narrowed his eyes. "Turn it over to me and you can be on your way back home."

She jutted out her chin and stepped forward. "Not on your life, Les! I promised to check into this and I mean to do it!"

Les's eyes snapped and he shook his head. "Don't get in my way, Red Pepper! I'm not Fritz Javor and I'm not overwhelmed with your looks like he would be."

Fire blazed from her blue eyes. "I didn't expect you to be!"

"Oh, didn't you? Didn't you think you could walk in here, blink those long lashes and shake all that red hair around so I'd do anything you wanted, get my help, and then tell me to butt out? Isn't that your plan, Red Pepper?"

Anger shot through her and she doubled her fists at her sides and squared her slender shoulders. "Thank you for your help, Chief. I'll let you know when I have Susie Archer located so that you can question her."

"Don't you hear well?" Les gripped her arm in a surprisingly tight hold. "You're out of this deal. I'll handle it from here on out. I'm head of the police in this town, and what I say goes. I don't much like private cops, especially red-headed ones."

"I have a case to solve and a client to protect, Les Zimmer, and I mean to do it!"

His nose almost touched hers and his breath fanned her face. "Want to bet on it?"

"It's a sure thing! I promised Carla my help and I'll give it to her. She doesn't need the police force to barge in on her life and warn Susie Archer that we're on to her. If I investigate quietly I'll learn where Susie is and I'll give you the pleasure of questioning her."

He shook his head. "No deal. You leave it alone or I'll find a way to stop you. Fritz Javor or not."

She grabbed up her purse from the chair. "I know my rights, Chief, so don't threaten me."

He grinned easily and lifted his hands, his arms bent at the elbows. "Is that what I'm doing, Red Pepper?"

"Don't call me that!"

He shrugged. "Why not, Red Pepper?"

Her brilliant red hair flying she whipped around and strode from the station to Peg's car parked next to an unmarked police car.

At the library she parked beside a blue Mustang, took a deep breath and walked inside. Peg was waiting in the reading room, her body charged with electricity.

Amber dropped down beside Peg and clutched her purse on her lap.

"What's wrong, Amber? You look ready to burst."

"Some people make me so angry!" Amber took another deep breath and shrugged out of her coat. Two women peeked in the reading room door, then walked away, talking quietly. Children laughed and chattered in the children's section. "At times I wish I could use my karate just for the pleasure of it. But let's not talk about that. What did you find?"

"I thought you'd never ask!" Peg slid to the edge of her oak chair. "Information about Mark Yonkers' accident. There was an investigation because of the brakes, but nothing came of it."

"Good work, Peg." Amber pushed back her hair.

"I found out that Bobby Archer died six years ago in Thornapple and was survived by one sister, Susie Archer."

"Oh, my!"

"Carla lived in Thornapple. Either she's lying about knowing Bobby and Susie Archer, or she didn't look far enough back into her past." She tapped Peg's arm. "I think it's time to visit Carla Reider again, don't you?"

Peg reached for her coat. "What about Lisa? What will you tell Carla about Lisa?"

Amber drummed her fingers thoughtfully on the table. "I will call Lisa's family in Texas and see if they know where Lisa is, then we'll talk to her and get it settled.

"Good idea."

Amber took out the phone number that Peg had given her, walked to the pay phone outside the library and dialed the number, her back against the icy wind.

"Dickon residence."

"Sir, this is Amber Ainslie. My cousin, Peg, works with Lisa Dickon and we're trying to reach her."

"Lisa Dickon? I'm sorry. You must have the wrong number."

Amber gripped the receiver tightly. "Lisa gave this number to my cousin and said she could be reached here."

"I'm sorry, but there's no Lisa here. Did you try the other Dickon family here in town?"

"No, could I have the number?" Amber jotted it down as the man gave it to her. "Thank you for your help. I'm sorry to inconvenience you." She hung up and turned to Peg questioningly. "She doesn't live at that address."

"That's strange. She gave me that number at

Thanksgiving time and I wrote it down because I was working on a story that she had started. She said if I needed help with it, to call her there."

"I'll try this number." Amber used her calling card and called the number. A woman answered in a soft drawl on the first ring. "I'm trying to reach Lisa Dickon. Is she there?"

"You have the wrong number, dear. Maybe you should call the other Dickon family here in town."

"I already did, and they gave me your number."

"I'm terribly sorry, but we have no Lisa here."

"Thanks for your time." Amber hung up and turned to Peg, her eyes wide with questions. "Why would Lisa give you an incorrect number?"

"I don't know! It's a shock to me. I never needed to call her, so I didn't find out that it was the wrong number." Peg gripped Amber's arm. "Do you think there is a chance that Lisa could really be Susie Archer?"

"I don't know, Peg." Amber pulled her coat tighter around herself and walked toward Peg's car in the library parking lot. "I think we'd better go talk to Carla."

In silence Peg started the car and drove out of the parking lot. "This is becoming quite a mystery, Amber. It's a good thing you're here to figure it out."

Amber turned her head away, then finally turned back to Peg. "Please, don't get angry or hurt, Peg, but I came here to solve this case."

Peg wrinkled her brow. "You did? I thought you came to visit me."

Amber moistened her lips with the tip of her tongue. "I did come to visit you, but I came because my case led me here. I'm sorry."

Peg drove in silence for a block while she thought it over. "I guess I can live with that. I'm just glad you're here. It would be a very dull Christmas without you." She smiled across at Amber and Amber smiled back, relieved that it was finally in the open. "Why didn't you tell me before?"

"I was afraid you wouldn't keep my reason for being here a secret."

"I might not have, but now that I know the importance of secrecy, you can trust me."

"I know. You're great, Peg. I guess I let myself forget."

"It's easy to do that. Now, if you could make peace with your dad, everything would be perfect."

"Peg!"

Peg chuckled as she turned onto Carla's street. "I couldn't let such a grand opportunity pass, could I?"

"I guess you couldn't. Amber leaned forward for a better look out the windshield. "Isn't that Peter sitting outside Carla's place?" She pointed to the blue Honda.

"It is Peter! I wonder why he doesn't go inside." Peg pulled up beside Peter's car and Amber rolled her window down.

She reached out and tapped on his window.

He turned a haggard face to her and rolled his window down. "What?"

"What's going on? Why don't you go inside with Carla?"

He rubbed an unsteady hand across his face. "She's still not home. I was here earlier. I looked in her garage and her car is still gone. I decided to sit here and wait until she comes back."

Peg saw his anguish and she leaned over to look across Amber to Peter. "You look like you need some cheering up, Peter. Why don't we all go have lunch? We'll come back after and by then Carla is sure to be home."

Peter shook his head. "I don't want to leave here. I am so afraid something terrible will happen to her!"

"Sitting here won't help her," said Amber softly. "She said I could come over late this morning to get something from her, so I'm sure she'll be back soon." He looked ready to collapse and Amber knew something hot to eat and drink would help revive him. "We could go grab a quick bite and be back within the hour. I have a couple of questions to ask you, and this would be a perfect opportunity."

He closed his eyes momentarily, then nodded.

"Ride with us," said Peg.

Peter climbed in the back seat and sat back with a troubled sigh. "I hope this is all a big misunderstanding, and Carla really isn't in danger."

Amber and Peg exchanged glances, but neither said a word.

Chapter 5

Amber stood with Peg beside Peter's Honda as she waited for Peter to walk back from checking the garage for Carla's car. From the droop of his wide shoulders and the haggard look on his handsome face she knew that the car was still gone. She sighed and pushed her hands deep into her coat pockets. Lunch hadn't gone well and she knew that what she'd told Peter hadn't reassured him at all. His report on his talk with Madge hadn't give Amber any more information that she could use, but she'd made a mental note to talk to Madge before the weekend was over.

Peter stopped beside Amber. "It's not there."

"Where can she be?"

"I wish I knew!"

"Peter, are you sure you want to wait here for Carla?" asked Peg with a worried frown. She hated to see him so tense and frightened.

"What else can I do?" He shivered against the wind.

"Go home and wait there," said Amber. "She might try to call you."

His brain whirled as he tried to decide the best plan of action. "Maybe I could do that. I could be back here in five minutes if . . . when she does come back."

"If we learn anything we'll call you immediately."
Peg touched Peter's arm. "I promise."

"Peg and I are going to try to talk to the others in
Carla's office to see if they can help," said Amber.
"But we will be in and out of Peg's place if you need
to reach us."

Peter looked longingly at Carla's house, then
slowly slid under the steering wheel of his car. How
he wanted to catch Carla up in his arms and run far
away with her, away from danger. He lifted a hand
to Amber and Peg, looked to see that nothing was
coming, and drove away.

"There goes a frightened man," said Amber with
a sigh.

"He really loves Carla," said Peg. "I hope she
appreciates him."

Amber nodded absently as she walked up the
sidewalk that led to Carla's front door. It was very
strange that Carla was still away when she knew
how important it was for her to read the story by
Susie Archer.

Just then a middle-aged man standing in the yard
next to Carla's called out, "Excuse me, Miss, but do
you think you could get Carla for me?"

Amber strode across the yard to the man, Peg
close beside her. "What did you say?" asked Amber.

The man lifted his collar to protect his neck and
ears from the cold. "I need to put my car in the
garage, and I want you to ask Carla to come and
take hers out."

Amber and Peg stared at each other, then turned
back to the man. "Did Carla put her car in your
garage? Why? When?" asked Amber over Peg's
same questions.

He nodded. "She said she wanted privacy this
morning and the only way she could get it was to

make people think she was gone. This morning early, she came over to ask if she could use my garage. Of course I said yes."

"We'll tell her to move it right away," said Amber.

"Tell her I need it moved now. I left my car out for almost three hours waiting for her to come over, but now I want to go watch the game on TV and I don't want to be disturbed."

"We'll see that she comes right over," said Peg, holding her blowing hair out of her face with a gloved hand.

"I'll wait in my car." The man walked to his Cadillac as Amber and Peg ran to Carla's door.

"What a strange thing to do," said Peg.

"I can't believe she didn't let us know." Amber pushed the doorbell and waited with her shoulders hunched against the wind. Peg shivered beside her, her nose pink.

Suddenly the door burst open and Carla stood before them, her eyes red-rimmed and wild, her face gray and her hair mussed. She gasped when she saw Peg and Amber, and frantically looked behind them. "I thought you were the police. I hoped you were!"

"Why? What's wrong?" Peg clutched Carla's arm. "What happened, Carla?"

Amber eased them inside and closed the door, blocking out the icy wind. "Are you expecting the police, Carla?" She recognized immediately that tension laced with fear filled the hallway. She had seen the same thing many times before. She could tell Carla was at the breaking point and she longed to say the right words to help her.

Carla shook her head to clear her brain, but still she couldn't focus on the situation. "The police should've come by now."

"Let's go sit down and talk about it," said Amber.

"Come on, Peg." With one on either side they led Carla to the quiet living room. At a glance Amber took in the scattered papers on the floor. She eased Carla to a rose colored chair. "Would you like to tell us why you were expecting the police?"

Carla looked helplessly at Amber. "The story. I read it."

Amber knelt beside the chair. "Carla, I can see that you're very distraught. I want to help you. Try to calm down and tell me about the story."

"You can't help me. Only the police can."

Peg leaned down to Carla. "Since the police aren't here to help, Amber can. Do you understand, Carla? Amber solves crimes and mysteries all the time."

Carla turned haunted eyes on Amber. Her brain whirled in confusion as she tried to decide where to start.

Amber waited quietly, silently praying for Carla. In her years as an investigator Amber had learned that skill and hard work put together with prayer brought great results.

Finally Carla nodded. "I'll tell you, but I still don't understand why the police didn't come. I called them and told them and they brushed me off."

Amber pushed herself up with easy grace, slipped off her coat and walked to the couch to sit down. "Peg, get Carla's car keys and get her car before her neighbor comes over."

"My car! Oh, yes, my car!" Carla picked up the keys from the coffee table. Peg took them and hurried out.

Amber waited until the door closed behind Peg. "What did you tell the police, Carla?"

Carla brushed an unsteady hand over her eyes. "Susie Archer is going to kill me."

"You told me about the threat. Did she call

again?" Amber kept her voice calm and low-pitched. She assumed the police hadn't come because they hadn't believed Carla, but she didn't understand why, especially after her talk with Les Zimmer.

Carla pointed to the scattered papers on the floor with a trembling finger. "It's all in there. Susie Archer's terrible story! It's awful!"

Amber picked up the papers, put them in order and sat back down. She read the title and the by-line as well as the first two pages, then she looked at Carla. "I assume you now remember who Bobby and Susie Archer are."

Carla nodded and tears welled up in her green eyes. With a halting voice she told Amber the essence of the story with questions now and then from Amber. "I don't know why Susie would blame me for Bobby's death, but she does. She . . . she called me. Or someone claiming to be Susie Archer called me." Her voice broke, but she finally continued to tell all she could remember of the phone conversation. "I'd like to think it's all a bad joke, but it doesn't sound like one at all!"

"This is unreal!" Peg hooked her blond hair behind her ears with an unsteady hand. She had come in quietly while Carla was talking and had watched and listened as they talked. Peg locked her hands together in her lap. How could Amber stay so calm in such a terrifying situation?

Amber studied the pages critically, then passed them over for Peg to see. "Carla, you say the story was tucked in with the others when you found it?"

"It was the fourth one in the pile and it didn't have a review sheet clipped to it. I was sure Lisa had written it."

"No review sheet? Is that unusual?"

"Very unusual." Some of the color returned to

Carla's cheeks. "My editors always use review sheets so that I know I'm reading something they recommend. But there wasn't one on that . . . story."

"I know I haven't seen this before," said Peg in a hushed voice. "And I'm sure the other editors haven't either. Yet it's typed in manuscript form and it was in the reviewed stack of stories."

Amber took the papers from Peg and studied them thoughtfully again. "I believe that someone with writing knowledge did this. I wonder where Susie Archer learned such skills? And Susie says, assuming that Susie herself wrote this, that she works with you, Carla. She could have put this story on your desk with the others without your knowledge. She has access to your desk."

Peg shivered at the thought.

Carla locked her icy hands together in her lap. "But I know everyone I work with."

"Then one of them put the story there."

Peg uncrossed her long legs and slid to the edge of her chair. A car honked outdoors. The furnace blower clicked on and hummed in the background. "I hate to think it's someone we know."

Amber bit her bottom lip and looked from Carla to Peg and back again. "There isn't any other explanation. Maybe the person didn't know what he or she put in the pile of stories." Amber narrowed her eyes thoughtfully. "Someone could have asked, as a favor, for the story to be slipped in with those." She pointed to the other stories on the coffee table in front of her. "We don't know if Lisa Dickon wrote it. I tried to call her, but couldn't get her."

"I don't think it was Lisa Dickon," said Peg firmly. "She's too nice. Besides, she has a Texas drawl that she couldn't have picked up here in Michigan."

"If Lisa is Susie Archer, she could easily fake a

drawl. I know you don't want to think that. You don't want to think badly of anyone you know. Yet, the story was in the pile." Amber rubbed her hand over her soft wool pants. "Someone put it there. Is it possible that Susie Archer works in your office? She said in her story that she looked different. Could she work for you and you not know it?"

Carla shuddered and wrapped her arms across herself. "I hate to think that. I know everyone working for me."

"So do I," said Peg. "None of them is a killer." The thought of someone in the office being a murderer sent chills up and down her back.

"Killers can be ordinary people," said Amber. she turned to Carla. "Is there anything about Susie Archer that you can remember? What does she look like? Does she have anything unusual about her speech? Can you think of anything?"

Carla narrowed her green eyes and tapped a long finger against her lips. "She was outspoken, sometimes loud and abrasive. She was overweight, greasy dark hair and brown eyes, and she dressed in overalls a lot."

"Doesn't anyone you know fit that description?"

"No."

Amber picked up a blue throw pillow and held it on her lap. "What happened to Susie Archer after Bobby shot himself?"

"I don't know. I was too involved with school and myself to think about Bobby or Susie." Carla tucked her hair behind her ears. "I was so self-centered!"

"How about your mother? Would she remember?"

Carla nodded. "She might."

"Give me her number and I'll give her a call." Amber walked to the phone and Carla told her the number to dial.

In a few minutes Zinnia Reidel was on the phone answering Amber's questions about Susie. She had a pleasant voice that sounded much like Carla's.

"It's been a long time, but I do remember that Susie had a mental breakdown after her brother's death. I don't know how long she was in the hospital and I don't know which hospital."

"I need to find out what hospital, Mrs. Reidel. Please, it's important."

"Won't you tell me what's wrong?"

"Carla will explain it all when she sees you for Christmas."

Mrs. Reidel cleared her throat. "Bobby shot himself Christmas day."

Amber's brain whirled. Bobby died at Christmas. Mark died at Christmas. And now threats to Carla were coming at Christmas. Was it possible that Susie would find a way to keep Carla in town so that she could shoot her Christmas day? Amber kept the panic out of her voice as she said, "Mrs. Reidel, thanks for your help."

"I'll find out what hospital and call you right back. I know someone who remembers details like that."

Amber walked away from the phone, stood at the front window, then turned and told Peg and Carla what Mrs. Reidel had said. "It's a good lead. It should help me locate Susie Archer, hopefully before the day is over."

"I can't believe any of this is really happening to me!" Carla jumped up and paced the room, once again going over the contents of the story as well as the phone calls.

Amber let her talk while Peg sat quietly re-reading the story.

The phone rang and Carla shrieked, then clamped her hand over her mouth and stared at the phone.

"It's probably your mother," said Amber, stepping to the phone. "I'll answer it." It was Zinnia Reidel and Amber listened as she went into great detail about Susie's breakdown and the institution that Susie Archer had been in, even giving the phone number of it.

"I could give you the name and number of the woman I talked to in case you need to know something more."

"Thank you, Mrs. Reidel." Amber wrote down the name and number, said goodbye and hung up. "Now, I'll call the institution." She dialed as she told some of what Mrs. Reidel had said. When a woman answered the phone, Amber quickly stated her name and business.

"I'm sorry, but I can't give out any information about the patients."

In frustration Amber gripped the phone tighter. "Who was her doctor?"

"I suppose it won't hurt to tell you. Wait just a moment while I check. It'll take a while."

"I'll wait."

Finally the woman came back to the phone. "Dr. James Everett."

Amber nodded. Susie had said her doctor was Dr. Everett. "May I speak to him?"

The woman sighed heavily. "He is just walking out."

"Catch him! Please. It's a matter of life and death!"

In a few minutes a man answered the phone, sounding tired and slightly impatient.

Amber smiled at Carla and Peg reassuringly, then quickly told the doctor her name and her reason for calling.

"Let me get back with you, Ms. Ainslie," he said. "I want to read my file before I say anything."

"Could you call yet this afternoon? It is urgent."

"Yes, I can see that. I'll call."

"Thank you!" Amber gave him Carla's number and she hung up and took a deep breath. "Now I think we should make a list of the people in the office and check them out. It's possible that someone from another office slipped the story in without anyone noticing, but we'll concentrate on the people you work with."

Carla stood quietly beside the coffee table deep in thought while Amber waited silently. "I hate to invade their privacy, but I can see it is necessary."

Amber nodded. "What about the police, Carla? Shall I call them and find out why they didn't come to investigate your report?" Amber saw the sudden panic in Carla's green eyes.

"No! I don't want the publicity this would make if it turns out to be nothing." Carla pushed a shaky hand through her sandy blond hair. "Or if, for some strange reason, it's all in my mind. This has been a very bad two years for me." She cleared her throat. "What if I wrote the story and made up the phone calls?"

Amber reached for Carla's hand. "You didn't make it up, Carla. You are not losing your mind. Trust me." Amber smiled reasuringly and the haunted look left Carla's eyes. "Now, how about a pot of tea before we sit down and write out that list? We'll keep busy while we wait for Dr. Everett to call back."

"Let me make the tea. It might help me to realize this is not just a nightmare." Peg looked from Amber to Carla and said just above a whisper, "I can't believe any of this! I can't believe you're really in danger."

"I can't either," said Carla as she pushed her hands into her jeans pockets and hunched her slender shoulders.

Amber shugged. "I've met a lot of strange people. This kind of thing does happen. It's better to check everyone and everything."

Peg held a pad of paper out to Amber. "I already started the list of the people we work with, Amber. I wrote down what I know about each one. It's hard to imagine any of them doing this to Carla."

"I'm sure it is." Amber scanned the list thoughtfully with Carla looking over her shoulder and adding information while Peg walked to the kitchen to brew the tea.

Several minutes later Peg brought in a tray with tea, cups, milk, sugar and a plate of Oreo cookies. She set them on the coffee table, then rubbed her hands up and down her arms. "Amber, I suddenly realized that if you weren't the investigator in this I'd be a suspect too, wouldn't I?

Amber nodded without looking up.

Peg ran a finger lightly around the rim of her cup. "I can't believe it's anyone I know."

Amber shifted her attention from the list Peg had written in the tidy handwriting that Amber knew so well. "You did a good job on this. You're very good with details, Peg."

"Thanks."

Carla picked up her cup of tea and leaned back on the couch next to Amber. "Is there a way you could meet with any of these people today or tomorrow?"

"I plan to. The sooner, the better."

Peg frowned thoughtfully as she absently sipped her tea. She set down the cup and nodded slightly. "Greg. Madge? Outside the office she won't speak to anyone she works with. Once I met her in the grocery store and she wouldn't say hello or smile or anything. I felt like ramming my cart into hers, but I restrained myself." Peg laughed, then continued.

"I've had lunch with Lisa a few times, and Kathy and I have shopped together. They aren't married either. Jane is married, so I see her only at the office."

"How about giving them a call? See if we can drive to their homes to talk to them. Tell them that I want to meet the people behind the magazine."

Peg nodded. "I'll try Lisa at her apartment again, too." She reached for the phone, then turned to Amber with a loud gasp. "We forgot to call Peter to let him know Carla is safe!"

Amber clamped her hand to her mouth. "And we promised!"

"Don't call him!" cried Carla. "I don't want him here! I don't want him involved in this!"

"But why?" Peg took a step toward Carla. "Peter loves you! He wants to be with you!"

"Don't you understand what it could mean? I loved Mark Yonkers and he was killed because of me. I don't want that to happen to Peter!"

Amber laid a hand on Carla's trembling arm. "Easy, Carla. It won't help for you to get hysterical. But I do think we should call Peter just to reassure him. He was afraid something terrible had already happened to you. Let Peg call him and she can tell him not to come here."

"He won't listen," whispered Carla. "He'll rush right over."

Amber and Peg exchanged looks and Amber turned back to Carla. "If Peter's here with you, you'll see that he's safe, won't you? And he'll see that you are. It might be better for both of you. Besides, we'd feel a lot better if you weren't alone while we're off seeing the office people."

Carla tucked her hair behind her ears and finally nodded. "All right. Call Peter." She frowned as she thought of the diamond ring that was in her purse.

She hoped he wouldn't bring that up.

Just as Peg reached for the phone it rang and she jumped back. Amber stepped forward to answer it.

"This is Jim Everett, Ms. Ainslie."

Amber sank to the chair near the phone table. "What did you find?"

"I'd rather talk to you in person. I'll be going through there on my way to Detroit. Could I stop and talk to you?"

A shiver ran down Amber's spine. "If you feel it's necessary."

"It is. I'll see you about seven tonight."

Amber gave him both Carla's and Peg's addresses and phone numbers. "If you can't find me at one place, try the other." After she hung up she turned to Carla and Peg. "He feels this is very serious, so he'll be here about seven."

"Oh, my," whispered Peg.

"I hope he can help," said Carla with a shudder.

Amber nodded as she walked away from the phone to leave it free for Peg to use. "Carla, can you remember anything else that would help me?"

"Like what?"

"Like strange happenings in the past few months. Anyone new in your life that could be Susie Archer. Or anything about Susie Archer that you remember that could help us identify her."

Carla shook her head. Right now she didn't think her brain would ever function correctly again.

Peg turned from the phone. "Peter is on his way. He was ecstatic to learn that you were safe, Carla."

The words warmed her more than she wanted to admit.

Peg turned to Amber. "I couldn't get Lisa or Jane, but Greg and Kathy are expecting us shortly."

"Good work, Peg."

"You girls don't have to wait here with me until Peter comes if you don't want to." Carla wanted to rush to the bathroom and brush her hair and repair her makeup before Peter came. "I know you're anxious to meet with Greg and Kathy."

Amber slipped on her coat, rolled Susie Archer's manuscript and tucked it in her pocket. "We'll see you later. I do think I'll stop by the police station before we return to see why they didn't answer your call, Carla. I think it's important too. There could be more to it than we know."

"If you think it's best," said Carla. She didn't want to think about involving the police, but she trusted Amber's judgment.

"Don't open your door to anyone except Peter," said Peg over her shoulder as they walked to the front door.

"I won't." Carla closed the door behind them, then dashed to the bathroom to brush her hair and apply a little makeup so she wouldn't look quite so pale and lifeless.

A few minutes later she opened the door to Peter's insistent knock, her heart pounding at the sight of him. Just seeing him brought her comfort. Without a word he stepped inside, pushed the door shut and took her in his arms. She stiffened, then clung to him as if she'd never let him go. He held her tightly to him with his face pressed into her smooth sandy blond hair. He smelled the clean smell of shampoo before he held her from him just enough to look into her face. "Darling, I had to come. I am going to stay with you as long as you'll let me. Nothing is going to happen to you! No one can harm you! I promise."

She studied his face, her eyes questioning.

"I mean it, Carla. I love you and I won't let anything happen to you."

She smiled a shaky, unsure smile. "Let's sit down. My legs are a little weak."

"I see you've been working on your stories. I admire you for keeping on with your work. You're quite a woman."

She smiled as they sat side by side on the flowered couch. "Thanks. I knew I couldn't stop working even with a threat on my life. It could prove to be nothing."

"I sincerely hope it does!" Peter pulled her close to his side and captured one of her hands in his. "I couldn't live without you, Carla."

"Oh, Peter!" She turned and pressed her face into his shoulder.

Several minutes later the phone rang and she jumped nervously.

"I'll answer it." Peter scooped it up before it had a chance to ring again. "Hello."

"Peter, this is Amber Ainslie. May I speak to Carla? It's important."

He held the phone out to Carla. "It's Amber."

Carla grabbed it and cradled it to her ear. "Yes?"

"We're at Greg's apartment and I suddenly thought of something that I should have thought of before. Do you have your old yearbooks? Ones that would have photos of Susie Archer?"

Carla's breath caught in her throat. Why hadn't she thought of that? "Yes, I do have some yearbooks. I'll hunt them up immediately."

"Great! Peg and I will be back as soon as possible. And Carla, if the police happen to come, don't say anything about the yearbooks or they'll keep them from me. You can tell them what you told me, tell them I have Susie Archer's story, but don't say anything about the yearbooks. I want to have a look at them before the police have a chance to take them

away. I don't know if they'll come see you, but they
might. Just stay calm and answer their questions. See
you later."

"I'll have the yearbooks ready." Carla hung up
and told Peter what Amber had said.

"Let's find the books," said Peter.

"They should be in the bookcase." She looked
over the shelves and finally found three old yearbooks that she hadn't looked at for years. A strange
feeling washed over her and she almost dropped the
books.

"Let's look at this Susie Archer," said Peter as he
took one of the books from her.

"She was three or four grades ahead of me. I think
she was a senior when I was a freshman." Carla
looked in the index of one of the books, but only
found Bobby Archer and not Susie. She flipped to his
picture and her stomach tightened as a bitter taste
filled her mouth.

"Here she is," said Peter. "She has a scowl on her
face. Do you remember her?"

Carla looked at the picture and slowly nodded.
"Brown hair and eyes, overweight, stayed to herself,
about my height."

"Have you seen her around here?"

"No! But I wouldn't really know if I did. She did
say in the story that she wears contact lenses now
and has dyed her hair, but I couldn't recognize her,
I'm sure."

"She looks very unhappy, doesn't she?" Peter
opened the book to another page where her picture
was displayed and Carla bent over to study it
closely. They talked about Susie and Bobby, and
Carla's relationship with them.

The doorbell rang and she jumped and dropped
the yearbooks in her hands. They fell at her feet.

"That's probably Amber."

Peter opened the door and Les Zimmer strode in, his wallet flipped open to show his badge, his face red from cold.

He shoved his wallet into the back pocket of his faded jeans. "Chief of Police Les Zimmer. I assume you're Carla Reidel?"

She nodded and looked helplessly at Peter.

"I'm Peter Scobey, a friend of Carla's."

Les nodded as he shot a quick look around the room. He saw the books on the lush carpet and as he looked pointedly at them Carla flushed and quickly scooped them up and dropped them on the coffee table. Peter laid the one he held on the table near the phone.

The doorbell rang again and Peter opened it before Carla could move. Amber walked in and stopped short when she saw Les Zimmer. She had tried to reach him after her visit to Greg, but he wasn't available.

He smiled smugly. "Hi, Red Pepper."

Anger rose in her, but she wouldn't let it show. "Hello."

"I thought I told you to stay out of this."

"You did, but I told you that I wouldn't."

"I came to question Carla Reidel and I don't want you here while I do."

"That's ridiculous! I already know everything about the case, Les. I won't get in your way."

"You're already in my way! Why didn't you bother to tell me that Carla Reidel called us this morning?"

"I was going to. Why didn't you bother coming before this?"

A muscle jumped in Les's jaw, but no other sign of discomfort or guilt showed. "I'm here now." He took a step toward Amber. "I want you out right now, Red. Got it?"

"You tell me why you didn't come sooner and I'll get out."

Les hesitated, then shrugged. "We got two calls this morning. Two calls from Carla Reidel."

"No!" Carla shook her head. "I called once about ten."

"The first call came about nine-thirty."

"Very interesting," said Amber. "What did the first caller say?"

Les hunched his shoulders. "She said that another call would be coming in from someone claiming to be Carla Reidel, but we should disregard it because it was a hoax."

"Well, well," said Amber, grinning at Les's apparent embarrassment.

"I didn't see the entry until just a few minutes ago. Of course, I came right over."

"Of course," said Amber with a chuckle.

"Get out of here, Red Pepper! Now! I have business to attend to. Without you." Les caught her arm and tugged her toward the door.

Amber glanced at Carla, down at the yearbooks, then allowed Les to escort her to the door. She didn't dare draw attention to the books or Les wouldn't allow her even a look into them. She walked out to join Peg in the car. Maybe they would go talk to Jane and then rush right back here.

Les drew out a pad, settled down on a chair and talked to Carla, getting all the details. He picked up the yearbooks and her heart stopped. He knew there was something she wasn't telling him concerning the books. He saw the date on them and hid a knowing grin. "Is there a picture of Susie Archer in one of these?"

Hesitantly Carla nodded and squeezed Peter's hand.

Les looked for the pictures, found them and nodded. "I'm taking these with me to show to the men in the department so we can be on the lookout for her." He looked toward the phone table, saw the other yearbook and scooped it up and added it to his pile while Peter and Carla groaned inwardly. He asked for a list of people she worked with and reluctantly she gave him names and addresses. "Now, what about the story that started all of this?"

"I don't have it."

His head snapped up. "Who does?"

Carla cleared her throat. "Amber Ainslie does."

"And where can I find her?"

"I don't know. You told her to leave. Remember?"

He stabbed thin fingers through his dark hair. "Where's she staying while she's in town?"

Carla told him and he walked out. She sank to the couch with her chin in her hands, her arms resting on her knees. "Now Amber won't have a picture of Susie Archer."

Peter caught her hand and held it firmly. "Don't you have another yearbook?"

"No."

"Not even at home?"

"No. And my brothers are younger than I am, so they wouldn't have anything with Susie's picture. What am I going to tell Amber?" Carla bit her bottom lip and blinked away hot tears.

Chapter 6

Peter tenderly kissed Carla's pale cheek. "Don't take it so hard, Carla. I saw the picture of Susie Archer. I could get our artist to draw one and then we could show that to Amber."

Hope lightened Carla's emerald eyes. "Great idea, Peter!"

"I'll give him a call right now." Reluctantly Peter pulled away from Carla to dial Joe's number. He waited, drumming his fingers on the telephone table, but Joe didn't answer. He hung up just as the doorbell rang again. Carla started for the door, but Peter stopped her with a gentle touch on her arm. "I'll get it."

Cold air rushed in with Amber and Peg, making the furnace kick on. "I saw the Chief leave, so we came back," said Amber breathlessly. "He didn't see us." She'd driven just around the corner and parked so that the second Les left she could come back. Anger at Les still simmered inside her and she wished that it hadn't been necessary to contact him.

Carla stepped forward with a gasp. "I forgot to tell him about the mental institution Susie was in and about the doctor coming here." Carla rubbed a damp palm down her jeans. "He did ask about Susie's story, and I told him all that I could remember. He wants it." Carla bit the inside of her bottom lip. "He also took the yearbooks, but Peter said maybe his artist could sketch a picture of Susie." She held a hand out to Peter and he clasped it warmly, giving her strength.

"I tried to call Joe, but he's not home." Peter led them into the living room. "I'll try him again in a few minutes."

"How about Kathy?" asked Peg. Her blue eyes flashed with excitement and her cheeks were flushed rosy pink. A fuzzy white hat covered her blond curls. "She does a lot of the artwork for *Woman's Life*. I think she'd help. We were just on our way to talk to her."

"Good idea," said Carla.

"Hold it!" Amber held out her hand and the others turned to look at her. "Do you know that you can trust her? Do you know that she is not Susie Archer?"

"She can't be," said Carla, shaking her head. "She is much too tall. Susie might've disguised herself, but she couldn't add a foot to her height."

"True." Amber nodded.

"Let's meet her at the magazine office." Peter slipped an arm around Carla. "She'll have all the materials there."

An hour later they stood in the deserted office around Kathy's desk as she sketched the picture of Susie Archer that Peter and Carla described. Kathy was almost six feet tall with black hair, flashing black eyes, and was reed thin dressed in jeans and a cream sweater.

"That looks perfect," said Peter with a nod.

"Now, draw one of her with a few years added to her," said Amber. "Maybe slim her down and give her a more mature hairdo instead of the long stringy hair that you gave her, and leave off the glasses."

Kathy nodded as she sketched on another paper.

Amber watched with interest and admiration as another picture appeared as if by magic from the tip of Kathy's drawing pencil. Amber glanced at each person around her. "Do you recognize her?"

"She looks like a lot of people I know," said Peg. "She's very ordinary looking."

"She is, isn't she?" said Carla with a disappointed sigh.

Kathy held her pencil poised as she looked up at Amber. "I wish you could tell me what hairdo to give her. That would make a difference."

"How about drawing a short one with more curls?" said Amber.

Everyone waited in silence as Kathy's pencil flew over the paper.

"You know, that looks like Madge, doesn't it?" whispered Peg.

Carla nodded, her nerves tingling.

"Let's go visit her right now," said Peter with an angry scowl.

"What is this all about?" asked Kathy. "You asked me odd questions about a girl named Susie Archer and had me draw these sketches, yet you won't explain."

"We'll explain everything as soon as we can," said Amber. "Sorry. I do need to ask you a couple more things." She hesitated a second while Kathy dropped her pencil back in the desk drawer. "Kathy, what do you know about Madge Eckert?"

Kathy shrugged a thin shoulder and pursed her full lips. "What does anyone know? She keeps to herself as far as I know."

"Let's go talk to her," said Peter again.

Amber agreed. "How about Lisa Dickon? Do you know where we can reach her, Kathy?"

"Sure. She went to Texas to be with her family."

"We called them and she's not there," said Peg. "They didn't even know anyone named Lisa Dickon."

Kathy chuckled as she slipped on her furry jacket. "You have to ask for Elizabeth Dickon. Elizabeth, not Lisa."

"Elizabeth? Her name's Lisa," said Amber.

"She calls herself Lisa," said Kathy. "She said she can't get her family to call her Lisa, and they won't respond if anyone else calls her that."

"I didn't know that," said Peg.

"I knew her name was Elizabeth, but I didn't think anything about it," said Carla. "I want to know if she put the story on my desk!"

"I think I'll give her a call now." Amber looked toward the phone on the desk Peg had said was Carla's and knew she'd have more privacy there than at Kathy's desk. "May I use your phone, Carla?"

"Yes, do!"

Amber walked away from the group, found the phone number in her purse and dialed it just as Peg joined her. When a man answered, Amber said, "May I speak to Elizabeth Dickon, please?"

"She's here. Just walked in the study. Elizabeth, it's for you."

Amber bobbed her eyebrows at Peg and whispered, "Lisa's there." Then to Lisa she said, "Hello, Lisa. I need a few minutes of your time, please. I'm Amber Ainslie, Peg's cousin."

"Oh, yes. She said you were going to visit her, but what do you want with me? How did you know to call here?"

"Peg gave me your number." Amber leaned back in Carla's chair. "Lisa, did you put your story in Carla's pile of manuscripts?"

"Never! I wanted to, but I didn't. Why?"

"Carla found a story in the pile and she thought you might have put it there."

"Well, I didn't."

"Did you put a story in the pile for a friend?"

"No!"

"Do you know if anyone else did?"

"No!"

"I want to know if you've ever been to Thornapple, Michigan."

"No. Why? What's going on? Why all the questions? Why did you bother to call me at home to ask all these strange questions?"

"Have you ever heard of Susie Archer?"

"No! What is going on!"

"It's all right, Lisa. Really. Here's Peg. She'll reassure you." Amber held out the white receiver and motioned for Peg to take it.

"Don't worry about this call, Lisa," said Peg in a rush. "We just had to check a few things for Carla. I'll tell you all about it when you come back."

"You sure everything's all right?"

Peg closed her eyes and leaned weakly against the desk. If only she knew! "Don't worry about a thing. Enjoy Christmas with your family. Is it warm there?"

"Heavenly! I'll try to bring some of it back with me when I come. I wish you'd tell me what's going on."

"I will when I see you. Enjoy your holidays. It's nothing that concerns you, Lisa. Really."

"If you're sure." She sounded uncertain. "Have a Merry Christmas, Peg."

Peg said goodbye and slowly replaced the receiver as she looked down at Amber. "Lisa is not Susie Archer," she whispered.

"You're right. Let's go talk to Madge, and then

Jane if we can reach her." Amber jumped up and walked to the others. "Carla, I talked to Lisa. She did not put a story in with the others."

"Then who did?" Carla's voice rose and Peter pulled her close to his side. Thankfully she leaned against him as she forced back her panic.

"I'd like to know who did it and why," said Kathy. "I'd like to know what's going on." She jutted out her chin and stood with her hands on her narrow waist as she looked from Carla to Amber and back again.

"When we know, we'll tell you," said Carla, sounding tired. "Thanks for your support. You're a good friend."

"I can't stand the suspense!"

"You'll help Carla a lot by not discussing this with anyone, not anyone, even if you trust them," said Amber.

Kathy nodded soberly.

Amber picked up the folder of drawings and led the way outdoors. Kathy called goodbye, her breath hanging in the crisp air, and dashed to her car with her coat collar up around her neck and ears.

The others stood outside the building, looking at each other questioningly. Cars drove past and holiday shoppers swarmed the sidewalks near the stores. Christmas music blared from loudspeakers half a block away.

Amber pushed a strand of flame-red hair out of her face. "We can't all burst in on Madge. I'll go alone and talk with her."

"We'll wait for you at Carla's," said Peter.

Amber drove Peg's car to the address Peter gave her, the city map open on the passenger seat. Madge's house was a duplex and she walked to the door that Peter had said was hers. A neighbor's dog barked. She knocked and waited, then finally Madge opened the door. She did indeed look somewhat like the picture, only her eyes were blue, not brown the way Carla had remembered Susie's.

"I'm Amber Ainslie, Madge. I need to discuss something private with you, if you don't mind."

"Ainslie? Peg's last name is Ainslie."

"I'm her cousin."

"What do you want with me?"

"Let's get in out of the cold so I can tell you."

Madge hesitated, then stepped aside for Amber to enter directly into the kitchen. From there Amber could see the front room and a door that probably led to the bedroom. Amber slipped out of her coat and hung it over a chair. She laid the folder on the kitchen table and opened it. "Do you recognize this woman?"

Madge sat down gracefully, motioned for Amber to follow, and pulled the folder to her. Madge was dressed in jeans that looked new, a white oxford shirt with a red sweater over it. Her rich brown hair shone with life and her face was made up very carefully, especially around her eyes. She looked at the sketches quickly, then shook her head and flipped the folder closed, "Should I know her?"

"I thought you might." Amber folded her hands over the folder. "Carla had an unauthorized story slipped in with the ones for the fiction contest. Do you know anything about that?"

"No. Should I? Peter said something about it. For some strange reason of his own, he wouldn't tell me anything about the story or why he was asking about it."

Amber sat back and crossed her legs, her eyes on Madge for every facial expression and body movement. "I understand that you don't like the idea of Peter Scobey seeing Carla."

"What? Where did you hear that?"

"From Peter."

Madge stuck her lips out in a pout. "I just don't want him to get hurt."

"You want him back for yourself, don't you?"

Madge's eyes flashed with anger and she lifted her chin. "It just so happens that I'm living with a man who loves me. I don't want Peter back. He never really cared for me."

"Then why did you call and insist Peter take you to dinner? And why did you call Carla to tell her about your dinner together?"

"What? I never! I didn't call Peter. I met Peter by chance and for old time's sake I asked him to take me to dinner. I did call Carla, but only because she doesn't treat Peter right." Madge shrugged. "Let Carla have him. I don't want him."

Just then someone knocked sharply on the door and Madge jumped up to answer it.

Les Zimmer strode in as if he belonged there and flipped his badge for Madge to see. "Madge Eckert?"

She nodded in a daze. "What going on here? Are you really the police?"

He nodded, then walked to Amber beside the table. "Don't you ever listen? I told you to butt out!"

She gathered up her coat and the folder. "I'll leave now, Les, but we're going to have to stop meeting like this." She smiled and he grinned, then scowled.

"About that story, Red Pepper."

"Yes?"

"I want it."

"I'll have to get it and bring it to your office later. Right now I have to run."

"Don't you have it with you?"

"No." It was safely tucked away in the car and not on her.

"What about this?" He snatched the folder from her hand and she grabbed for it, but he held it out of her reach and opened it. "Drawings. My, my. Susie Archer."

"Who's Susie Archer?" asked Madge, and Amber groaned for fear Madge was Susie Archer and now would be warned.

"The woman I'm looking for," said Les. "Do you know her?"

"Never heard of her."

To Amber, Madge looked as if she was telling the truth, but Amber knew she couldn't go by that. She snatched the folder from Les. "I'll see you later."

He stepped briskly between her and the door. "If you're not in my office before five with that story, I'll come pick you up and you won't like that much at all."

"You'll get the story, Les. By five." Amber stepped around him and strode out, fighting against her anger and frustration. Les was going to ruin her investigation, and probably warn Susie Archer that they were onto her plan. Amber slapped the steering wheel and shook her head. Her bright hair bounced around her shoulders. "How am I going to stay ahead of that man?"

She drove carefully, but quickly to a pay phone to try again to reach Jane Varden. She couldn't take the time for Peg to go with her. She had to question Jane before Les Zimmer did. Les was following the same list that she had, and Jane's name was last on it. Surely he hadn't found her home to talk to her yet.

A man answered the phone and Amber asked, "Is Jane home?"

"Yes, but she's down in the laundry room right now."

Amber's pulse leaped and she grinned. One more

for her side! "I want to drop over to see her for a
short time if it's all right. I'm Amber Ainslie. Jane
works with my cousin Peg and I want to meet all the
people working on the magazine while I'm in town.
I promise not to stay long."

"I'm sure she'll be pleased to meet you. She's
always talking about the people at work."

"See you in a couple of minutes then." Amber
drove quickly to Jane's house. It was a small house
not far from Peter's apartment. A bright red cardinal
flew from the bare branch of a maple tree and disappeared from sight around the house. Piles of dirty
snow stood near a row of bushes. Amber admired
the Christmas wreath as she knocked on the door. It
was opened immediately by a barrel-chested man
with thinning brown hair and a pleasant smile. He
wore faded jeans and a plaid flannel shirt with the
tails hanging over his jeans. Amber thankfully
stepped inside out of the cold and Don took her coat
and hung it in the closet as he introduced himself.
From where Amber stood she could see into the
small cheery kitchen with the counter and two tall
stools pulled up to it. An open doorway led down a
hall that probably led to the bedroom and bathroom.

"Jane's brushing her hair, but she'll be right out.
Have a seat." With a large, work-roughened hand he
motioned to the couch and a chair nearby.

The room was decorated with a pleasant mixture
of colonial and French Provincial furniture. Several
throw pillows stood in the corners of the couch. A
fire blazed in a Ben Franklin fireplace in front of a
brick wall. A large wicker basket held several logs
cut to size for the stove. The smell of the wood fire
was pleasant to Amber and she settled back in the
chair and crossed her long legs. Her dark pants
brushed against her leather boots. Her purple silk

blouse clung to her body attractively, but she saw that Don only had eyes for the woman who walked into the room. Jane had short light brown hair, fluffed around her slender face, brilliant blue eyes and an average looking face and figure. She wore dark slacks and a pink bulky sweater that looked very warm on such a cold winter day. She looked like Kathy's drawing of Susie Archer too. Amber forced back a disappointed sigh and stood as Don introduced them, his voice softening as he said his wife's name.

"Peg's cousin?" Jane tilted her head and studied Amber. Her voice was soft and pleasant. "You don't look much alike, do you?"

Amber laughed. "No, not much. I am a throwback from the fighting Irish in past generations." She sat down again as Jane and Don sat side by side on the couch, his arm around her slender shoulders. "I hope you don't mind my intrusion on your Saturday, but I did want to meet the people Peg works with." Amber smiled and crossed her legs. "I already met Carla Reidel. Very nice woman. Don't you agree?"

Jane nodded, but didn't say anything.

"Jane's always talking about her," said Don. "I've met her twice, and I like her."

"She asked me do her a favor since I was going to be here." Amber watched Jane very closely. Had she stiffened? "Carla found an unauthorized story in the pile of fiction that she's reviewing this weekend for the contest. Did you put it there?"

"Me?" Jane touched her chest with her finger tips and lifted her fine brows. "Of course not."

"My Janie has been working on a story of her own for weeks now," said Don proudly.

"Don!" Jane's voice was sharp, then she smiled.

"Amber doesn't want to hear about my budding talent."

"I'm interested in writing," said Amber. "What kind of story are you writing?"

"None that will sell, I'm sure."

"Don't put yourself down, honey. You can do anything you want to do if you work at it. Don't you agree, Amber?"

Amber nodded. She leaned forward and handed Don the folder. "Do you recognize the woman in the drawing?"

Don opened the folder and looked at the sketches. Jane studied them carefully and they both looked up at the same time. "I don't know her," they both said in one voice.

"Who is she?" asked Don.

Amber took back the folder, her mind whirling. She might as well come right out and ask since Les Zimmer was hard on her trail. He'd mess up everything for her anyway. "It's a drawing of Susie Archer."

"I don't know a Susie Archer," said Don. "Do you, Jane?"

Jane shook her head. "Should I?"

"I suppose not," said Amber. "I just thought I'd ask. She came from Thornapple. Have either of you ever been there?"

"No," said Jane.

"Yes," said Don. "Passed through a couple of years ago. Why?"

"Both Susie Archer and Carla Reidel came from Thornapple. Carla would like to get in touch with Susie." Amber stood up with easy grace. "I'd better get back to my cousin before she wonders if I got lost. We're planning Christmas dinner. Are you having dinner with your families?"

"Jane doesn't have a family and mine live in

Oregon," said Don. "We're going to enjoy our own Christmas, just the two of us. Jane bought a ham special for us. She knows how much I like ham. Don't you, Sugar?"

Jane smiled up at him, her face full of love, and nodded.

Amber talked a few minutes longer, then walked out. Was Jane Varden really Susie Archer? Like Madge, she was the right age and coloring except both women had blue eyes, not brown. Amber started the car and shook her head impatiently.

Would she find Susie Archer before she killed Carla? Amber's stomach tightened into an icy knot and she quickly pulled away from the curb. A block down the street she saw Les's unmarked car and she waved. He saw her but didn't wave back and she laughed.

She stopped at a stop sign and touched the story Susie had written. How was she going to get out of giving the only copy to Les? "I'll copy it!" She nodded and pulled ahead, laughing. She drove until she found a quick-copy sign. She tucked the story into the folder with the sketches and dashed for the print shop. Several minutes later she walked out with copies of the story and the sketches. Les could take everything and she'd still have a copy to show Dr. Everett when he arrived. She drove directly to the police station, dropped off the story with instructions to give it to Les the second he entered the door, then drove back to Carla's, upset that she didn't have anything positive to report.

At seven o'clock Amber paced the floor, silently praying while Carla, Peter and Peg sat in the kitchen over coffee and apple pie that Carla had bought from the freezer section of the grocery store. Carla had fixed them sandwiches for a snack, but no one had been able to eat much.

The doorbell rang and Amber dashed to the door,
took a deep breath and flung it wide. A well-dressed
man stood there, briefcase in one hand, his hat in the
other. "Dr. Everett?"

"Yes."

"Come in. Please! I'm Amber Ainslie." She closed
the door after him, took his coat and hat to hang in
the closet, and turned to find the others crowding
the hallway. "Dr. Everett, this is my cousin Peg,
Carla Reidel, and Peter Scobey."

He shook hands all around, his hand soft and
white and square. "I've heard your name, Ms. Reidel,
from Susie Archer. I'm sorry that I couldn't help her
when she was with me. It's a sad circumstance that
brings us together."

Carla led the way to the living room and they all
sat down, the doctor on the rose colored chair, his
briefcase beside him on the floor. He wore a well-cut
gray three-piece suit, a crisp white shirt, red, black
and gray striped tie, and black leather shoes pol-
ished to a mirrored shine. His dark eyes were alert
and seemed to take in everything at once. He
smoothed down his thinning gray hair and cleared
his throat.

"So, Susie Archer is trying to kill you, Carla? You
don't mind if I call you Carla, do you?"

"No." Carla bit her bottom lip and trembled, "I
thought, I hoped it was a hoax, a practical joke or
something, but I'm afraid it isn't. She called and she
wrote a story so that I'd know that she is going to
shoot me. She said she wanted me to suffer as much
as her brother did."

"Here's the story," said Amber. He took it as she
thought of the phone call from Les Zimmer about
two hours earlier concerning the story.

"I'd like to skin you alive for not showing me this

story when you first talked to me," Les had growled.

She'd managed to stay calm. "I already explained that I didn't have the story then, nor did I know the importance of it."

He was quiet a long time. "You tell Carla Reidel that I got a man on her house."

"I'm sure she'll be glad to hear that."

"I talked to the people on the list and got nowhere. How about you, Red Pepper?"

She gripped the phone tighter and her blue eyes flashed with anger at the nickname. "I didn't learn anything either." Should she tell him about Dr. Everett's visit? She shook her head and decided to wait and share any news afterward. If Les learned the doctor was coming, he'd question him and not leave any time for her to talk to him. He'd explained that he had only a short time to spend in Laketown, but wanted to read Susie's story and trade information in order to help find Susie Archer before it was too late.

"I do think that it would be better to be more discreet with your questions. We don't know now if Susie Archer will go into hiding so that we'll never find her. Carla might have this hanging over her head for a long time."

He yelled at her that he would do his job the way he saw fit. "And I don't want you getting in my way. Do you understand me, Red Pepper?"

She forced back her frustrated thoughts of Les Zimmer and focused her attention on Dr. Everett.

He looked up from reading the story, his narrow face grave. "This is indeed very serious. She means every word. Carla, I know that you once were Bobby's steady girlfriend because of the many talks that I had with Susie Archer, but I didn't know she still held destructive feelings toward you. I thought, indeed hoped, that she was past that." Dr. Everett tapped his briefcase. "I have her file here with a picture of her."

"May I see her picture?" Amber sat on the end of the couch near the doctor's chair with Carla beside her and Peter on the other side of Carla. Peg sat on the chair facing the doctor with her hands locked over her crossed knees. Shivers ran up and down Amber's spine as she watched the doctor open his briefcase and pull out a colored photograph. Would she be able to look at the picture and recognize the girl as someone she had met yesterday or today?

"You must remember that this was taken about four years ago." Dr. Everett held the picture out to Amber and she took it and studied it with a sinking heart as he continued to talk. "Susie Archer was a disturbed young lady and it shows in the picture. She was unkempt and overweight and very unhappy. She had loved her brother, and she couldn't get over the loss. It seems that she's still not over it."

"What did you want to tell us about her?" asked Amber, handing the picture to Carla.

"While she was with us she was determined to kill the girl she felt was responsible for her brother's death. That would be you, Carla. When Susie realized that she could not leave the hospital until she was rational she changed her story. She said that Bobby had killed himself because he was unhappy and couldn't face life, that only he was to blame. Susie said that she would not think about avenging his death, that she knew it was wrong. I knew in my heart what she was doing, but I didn't press her, and I'm sorry to say I allowed her to leave before she should have. She does want to kill you, Carla." Dr. Everett leaned forward. "And I believe she is planning to do it Christmas morning. That's when Bobby shot himself. From reading over her file and this story, plus hearing about the phone calls, I think that she will choose that time for the ultimate revenge."

Carla shivered and moved closer to Peter. "We must find her and stop her!"

"Yes," whispered Amber. How she wanted to leap to her feet and fly off to wherever Susie was hiding and stop her! Not knowing where Susie was, was setting her teeth on edge.

Dr. Everett crossed his leg and ran a finger and thumb over the sharp crease in his pants. "From the facts you've told me and the story, I also feel that Susie is crying out to be stopped. She is ridden with guilt over killing Mark Yonkers, and she knows she should be punished for it. She desperately wants someone to learn her identity and stop her.

"Then why doesn't she step forward and ask for help?" asked Peg with a frown. She gripped the arms of the chair as she helplessly stared at the distinguished looking doctor. Another few days of this and she would be ready for a long stay at the same hospital. How did Amber survive this kind of life? Peg glanced at her cousin and saw the tired droop to her shoulders and the dark smudges under her eyes. Would they have another sleepless night tonight?

"She would never do that because of the struggle going on inside herself."

"Doctor, isn't there anything about her that might help us identify her?" asked Amber.

He narrowed his dark eyes thoughtfully. "I noticed Susie had a tiny scar the shape of a V on the inside of her left wrist. Does that help at all?"

Carla slowly shook her head. "I never noticed a scar on anyone that I know."

"Nor I," said Peg.

"It's probably too small to notice unless you're really looking," said Peter.

"It is. I wish I could help with more information."

"What effect will it have on Susie to know that the police are looking for her?" asked Amber.

"The conscious part of Susie will be very angry and force her to be more determined, but the subconscious part of her will be relieved and even hopeful that she'll get caught."

"I want Carla to leave here," said Peter. "She can stay with me until Susie is caught."

"No!" Carla shook her head and her sandy hair slipped back and forth in a smooth swish. "I won't have this hanging over me! If I stay here, Susie will come to me and be caught. Amber as well as the police will see to that. Doctor, do you think I'm right?"

"It is up to you. I can understand your feelings, and I do think it's better to force Susie out in the open. It might be wise to let a trained policewoman stay here in your place. She will be more capable of handling Susie."

"Do that, Carla. Please!" said Peter.

Carla shook her head. "No! I must see this through. I will stay here. Susie won't try anything until Christmas morning according to the doctor, and the police will have me under constant protection."

A muscle jumped in Peter's jaw. "I'm going to stay here with you again tonight," he said hoarsely.

"That's wise," said Dr. Everett. "Susie is probably watching your house and she'll know that you're being protected. It might make her so angry that she tips her hand with some rash act."

"Do you think that tomorrow Carla will be safe?" asked Amber.

"Yes, I do." Dr. Everett looked from Amber to

Carla. "Susie wants you to suffer in fear before she confronts you."

"She's got her wish," whispered Carla.

"We know two women who have the general description of Susie with the extra weight off," said Amber slowly. "But both of them have blue eyes and not brown."

"Contact lenses," said Peg with rising excitement. "Amber! Colored contact lenses! We see them a lot!"

"Yes!" cried Carla, nodding. "Madge or Jane could wear colored contact lenses. But could either of them be Susie Archer?"

"Does either have a V-shaped scar on the inside of her left wrist?" asked Amber. "Peter? Does Madge?"

"I don't know. But I will certainly find out as soon as possible."

"We can't do anything tonight or tomorrow," said Amber. "Les Zimmer told me earlier that he learned that Madge and her boyfriend, Jane and her husband, and Kathy are going to be away for the day. We'll have to wait until Monday morning to visit them again." Amber turned from Peter to Dr. Everett. "Are you sure about Christmas morning?"

"Very sure. But there is always a possibility that I'm wrong. From my time with Susie and from reading this story, I think that she will try to kill Carla Christmas morning."

"Then we do have a little breathing space," said Amber. "It gives us more time to find Susie Archer."

Dr. Everett stood up with lithe grace and the others quickly stood. "I'll call you to learn of further developments."

"Thank you for coming," said Carla.

"I wish I could help more." He shook hands all around, slipped on his coat and hat and walked out into the cold, snowy night.

Susie Archer curled in the corner of the couch with the afghan over her legs and stared at the shotgun over the closet door. Would *they* stop her before she could shoot Carla Christmas Eve morning before she left for Thornapple? Susie moaned and leaned her head back. Things were getting too complicated with Amber Ainslie plus the police chief asking her so many questions. Had she given herself away when Amber Ainslie showed her the sketches? The one looked very much like she had when she was eighteen. But it was entirely different from her looks now. No one would recognize her as that unkempt girl.

"Coming to bed, sweetheart?"

She looked up and smiled. "In a minute honey."

"You've been very quiet since the Chief of Police was here. He was very interested in your shotgun until I told him that we never had shells in the house and that you wouldn't know how to load it if you tried."

She let him think that. She didn't want him to know that she had shells hidden in a bag under the front seat of the car behind a rag. And she did know how to use the gun; Bobby had taught her years ago and she practiced through the years so she wouldn't forget.

"I wonder if Amber Ainslie noticed the gun and didn't say anything. She sure was full of questions, wasn't she?"

Susie nodded and hid her trembling hands under the afghan that she'd crocheted a few months ago. "I'm tired of talking about her and the policeman and everything. Let's talk about what we're going to do tomorrow." She'd wanted a very special day with him just in case things went wrong Monday and she never got to see him again.

He dropped down beside her and kissed her long and hard. "We're going to do a lot of that," he whispered against her soft hair.

She laughed, then the laugh died in her throat. If he ever found out who she really was, he might never kiss her again. He must never learn that her real name was Susie Archer.

Chapter 7

Sunday morning Carla woke slowly, then sat bolt upright. An icy band squeezed her heart and her breath caught in her throat as she remembered the terrible threat on her life. Dr. Everett had said that Susie Archer was indeed capable of killing her, even though she was crying out in her own way for someone to find her and stop her. He felt that Susie was one of the women who worked with her. Carla gripped the edges of her sheet and covers. Maybe she should have agreed to go home early to stay until after Christmas. As much as she appreciated her mother's offer, she couldn't put them in danger. Susie would follow her to Thornapple if necessary. She dare not let that happen. She must stay here and face her and be done with it! Her family need not know that she was staying because of a death threat. If she ran now, Susie would only follow her. Susie had to be caught and stopped. They had to find her! Carla trembled and dropped back on her pillow. She was glad she had kept it from her parents. They wouldn't worry about her. Hopefully, Amber would find Susie and stop her. Shivering, Carla clutched the covers and groaned. As much as she wanted to believe everything would work out, she had her own private doubts. Maybe she *had* been to blame for Bobby's death. Maybe she deserved Susie's anger and hatred. Bobby had loved her and she should have been kinder to him. He might be alive today if she hadn't tossed him aside as easily as she'd tossed out her worn gym shoes.

Tears pricked her eyes as she eased out of the wide bed and slipped a burgundy velour floor-length robe over her soft pink flannel and lace night-gown. Dark circles underlined her eyes and her usually tidy sandy blond hair was mussed and dull looking. She knew Peter was still asleep in the other room and she didn't want to wake him. He stayed up late last night, pacing her living room while she forced herself to read her fiction.

With a low groan she picked up the pile of stories from the floor and carried them to the corner table near the window. She pulled the drapery aside and peeked out to see the sun trying to shine through the gray sky. Lazy snowflakes fell slowly on the yard and street. Dropping the curtain back in place, she eased into a chair and arranged the stories according to their potential. She had three more stories to read, then several to reread. Thoughts of the horrors of the last two days tried to intrude, but she refused to dwell on them. It was useless to be absorbed with her problems since she was helpless to solve them. She wrinkled her nose, knowing it was easier said than done. But she did have Amber. Amber was trained to solve crimes and mysteries. How she needed Peter to once again reassure her!

Longingly, Carla looked at the closed bedroom door as she pushed her hands deep into the pockets of her robe. She would not wake Peter, not this early on a Sunday morning. Just hearing his voice would help her, but she knew how badly he needed his rest. She sighed. Why hadn't she realized how much he'd come to mean to her? She loved him. Not the way she had loved Mark. He had been her whole life, and that kind of love only came once, but she did love Peter.

Taking a deep, unsteady breath she picked up a story, read a line, then dropped it back in place and jumped up, her icy hand trembling at her throat. She would shower and dress first; then maybe she could concentrate on her work.

"Dear God, how can this be happening to me?" A sob escaped and she dashed to the bathroom to hide in the shower.

Amber paced Peg's kitchen, her hands locked behind her back, her brain whirling with all the details about Susie Archer. Peg was still asleep after their late night. An uneasy feeling filled Amber and she sank to a chair and covered her face with her hands. Quietly she prayed for guidance and wisdom and for help with the Archer case. God was the head of her business and He knew all things. He knew where Susie Archer was and would help find her before Carla was harmed in any way.

The wall phone rang and she jumped up and grabbed it before it woke Peg. "Hello." Her voice was low and tense for she didn't know who to expect on the other end.

"I want to speak to Amber Ainslie."

Amber stiffened. "Good morning, Les. You sound chipper this morning."

"Stow it, Red! I want to know about the man you talked with at Reidel's house last night."

"It's Sunday morning, Chief. Early Sunday morning. Can't your business wait until later?"

"Not on your life, Red Pepper! Start talking."

She settled back on her chair and leaned an elbow on the table. Her hair, still damp from the shower, hung down over her thick terrycloth bathrobe. "His name is Dr. James Everett and he was Susie Archer's psychiatrist." With several interruptions from Les, Amber told him what she'd learned.

"I oughta run you out of town, Amber Ainslie."

"You should have let me handle this my own way, Les Zimmer. I wanted to take Susie Archer unaware, but you rammed your way in and made that impossible."

"We're never going to agree, Red, so let's drop it. So, you say Susie Archer does work in Reidel's office. You say she has a scar on her left wrist. Too bad I didn't know this when I talked to Reidel's office workers. Tomorrow I'll talk to them again and this time I'll look for the scar. And, Red, don't get in my way!"

"I will not drop the case, Chief!"

"You're impossible!" He slammed the receiver down and she hung up, frowning.

"I can't imagine why I make him so angry," she muttered.

"Who called?" asked Peg from the doorway, belting her pink robe and holding back a yawn.

Amber spun around. "I didn't know you were awake."

"I heard the phone. Who was it?"

"Les Zimmer." Amber wrinkled her nose. "He does not want me around, Peg, and sometimes I think I should just walk away from all of this and let him handle it. If it wasn't for my promise to Julie Kadau and to Carla too, I would."

"You need a cup of hot tea." Peg walked to the sink and filled the teakettle, set it on the stove to boil, then turned back to Amber. "Did you sleep at all last night?"

"Not much."

"You can't go on like this!"

She shrugged. "Peg, I wonder if Lisa Dickon has a V-shaped scar on the inside of her left wrist."

Peg's brows shot up to her mussed blond hair. "Amber! I thought you agreed that she couldn't be Susie Archer. Besides, she's in Texas."

"Since Susie isn't going to kill Carla until Christmas morning that gives Lisa plenty of time to hop a plane, waltz in and shoot Carla, and fly back to Texas. I've heard of stranger things happening."

"I think you're going wild all at once. What happened to your cool thinking brain?"

"I can't rule out anyone from the office except Kathy, because she's too tall, and Greg, because he's a man."

"Unless he's a woman dressed like a man."

Amber laughed. "I don't think he is, Peg. Stop teasing me. Lisa could be Susie Archer just as much as Madge or Jane."

"Lisa has blue eyes but she is the right age and all." Peg shook her head hard. "No! I will not believe it's Lisa!"

"We have to keep an open mind, Peg. If we let down our guard, we might not be able to stop Susie."

"What a grim thought! Of course you'll stop her! You're good."

Amber chuckled and hugged Peg. "You're a great cousin, Peg Ainslie. It's too bad Susie Archer didn't have a cousin like you to see her through her bad times."

Peg nodded. "Look what bitterness and unforgiveness can do to a person."

Amber laughed. "Peg, is there a message in there for me?"

"Yes. Yes, Amber, there is." Peg gripped the back of a kitchen chair and looked squarely at Amber.

"You can't let bitterness and unforgiveness toward your dad harm you."

Amber stood very still as she considered what Peg had said. Finally she nodded. "I know, Peg. I guess I've always known, but I didn't want to do anything about it." She turned away and looked at the dishes in the sink and the plant hanging at the window. Tears blurred her vision as she struggled with her emotions.

"I love you, Amber," whispered Peg. "I always want the very best for you."

"I know, and I thank you for it." Her voice broke. "I guess it is time to let go of those destructive feelings, but it's hard."

Peg rested her hand lightly on Amber's arm. "You don't have to do it alone; you have God's strength and love to help you. I'm right here, too, praying. We could pray together."

"Thanks, Peg." Amber clasped Peg's hands, then silently prayed for God to forgive her for harboring unforgiveness and bitterness in her heart, and asked for help to forgive Dad. Finally she lifted her face and smiled shakily. "I forgive him, Peg."

Tears sparkled in her blue eyes as Peg hugged her hard. "I think he'd like to hear it. Why don't you call him? And call your mother, too. I know she's been concerned."

"I guess I'd better call Dad before I back out." Amber reached for the phone with a steady hand and butterflies fluttering in her stomach.

Carla glanced at the clock just as she slid the bacon and cheese omelet onto the heated plate. Peter had said that he could shower and change at his house and be back in twenty minutes. She managed a shaky smile, knowing she could trust him to keep his word. Probably he'd even be back a couple of minutes early. She must stop worrying about Susie Archer walking through the door to shoot her. Dr. Everett knew what he was talking about, and he said that Susie wouldn't try anything until Christmas day. Until then she could relax. Her hand trembled as she poured steeped tea from the flowered pot into the yellow mugs and set them in place. She stood back to admire the table that she'd carefully set for them. A bud vase with one long-stemmed red rose stood to the side of the table to make room for the glass containers of jellies and jams in the center. The bright color of orange juice as well as the yellow cups and napkins made the table look festive. Peter would like the arrangement and the omelet. She held her finger to her cheek and tilted her head. It was really strange that danger to her had brought them so close together. Maybe she could learn to love him enough to marry him and live with him for the rest of her life. Her stomach fluttered and she whipped around at the sound of his knock on the door. She ran to open it for him. He pulled her close and kissed her as if he would never let her go. He smelled of fresh, cold air as well as after-shave lotion. He'd changed into dark brown cords, white shirt and a medium brown sweater that made his eyes seem darker.

"I missed you," he whispered gruffly.

"Breakfast is ready," she said in an unsteady voice.

He kissed her again, hung his leather jacket in the closet next to her coats, then walked to the kitchen to eat. If he had his way they would be married before the new year and never have to live apart again. He could bring so much happiness into her life that she'd forget her past.

She watched him over the top of her glass and

pictured him always sitting across the table from her. Her pulse leaped with excitement at the thought.

After he finished the orange juice and omelet she poured coffee for both of them. They walked to the living room to sit on the couch.

"I saw the man guarding your place, Carla. I feel easier with him there, but also strange to think that ordinary people like us have something like this happening."

"I'd give anything to go back to the way it was!"

Absently Peter rubbed his thumb across the knuckles of her hand. "Before me or before Mark?"

She stiffened. "That's not a fair question."

"You're right. Maybe it would be fair to ask if you're going to be able to put Mark completely into the past once this is over?" He couldn't bring himself to think that possibly the ending would be Carla's death. If he had anything to do with it, she'd live to be 103. "Do you think you could put him in the past?"

She turned slightly and cupped his cheek in her hand. How could she answer his question? Mark had been a part of her life for a long time, and it was hard to imagine him forever out of her thoughts. "Peter, you're a wonderful man. I do care about you. You know that. You've been my strength through this whole ordeal."

"Only because I forced myself on you."

She lowered her thick lashes, then lifted them again to look into his eyes. "I'm glad you did. You knew better than I did that I needed you, that I still need you."

He took her in his strong arms and kissed her until she could only think of him. Finally he held her from him. "Carla, maybe you should get away from here. I am afraid for you!"

Chills ran up and down her back. "I have been living with this threat over my life for a long time without even knowing it. Now that I know it, I want it stopped! I must do what I can to stop it! I must, Peter!"

"Shhh. Easy." He gently touched a finger to her lips. He saw the fear in her eyes and savage anger at Susie Archer burned inside him. What could he do to find her? Was it Madge? A band squeezed his head and he pulled Carla close and held her fiercely to him.

Amber had said that none of the suspects would be available again until Monday. But if they were, he'd go from one to the other until he learned who Susie Archer was and then he'd strangle her with his bare hands!

Carla felt Peter shudder and she rubbed her hands up and down his back. "Peter, you're too good to me. I don't deserve your love. I don't deserve you."

He drew away from her and chuckled, his dark eyes twinkling. "I'll remind you of that on our fiftieth wedding anniversary."

"Oh, Peter." She laughed with him, and it felt good after the hours of tension that had passed and that were still ahead.

Don stood over the bed and woke Jane with a kiss on each closed eye, the tip of her nose and her parted lips. "Wake up, sleepyhead. You have stayed in bed long enough."

She rubbed her hand up and down his arm. "Come back to bed."

He shook his head and laughed. "No way! Did you forget our great plans? We have places to go and things to see on this beautiful winter morning."

She touched his face tenderly and realized that he'd just shaved. He turned his head so that his lips touched the palm of her hand. She smelled the clean smell of soap on his skin. Nobody was as lucky as she. This man loved her in a way that she'd never known existed. She smiled dreamily. "Did it snow during the night? We ordered snow, remember?"

He nuzzled her neck, than stepped back from the bed. "It did snow. Just for us. So we have to take advantage of it."

She sat up slowly, lazily, and held out her arms to him. He scooped her close and lifted her against him.

"I love you," she whispered, then louder. "I love you more than I've ever loved anyone in my whole life!"

He kissed her long and passionately, then swatted her bottom and said, "Grab a shower, dress warm and let's go. We're going to breakfast and then on a long sleigh ride in the country. After that we'll go out for dinner and then cross-country skiing just like we planned."

"Just like we planned!" She laughed gaily and ran to the shower.

Madge sat with her back against the headboard of the bed with her knees pulled up to her chin. Tears streamed down her ashen cheeks as Tom slammed out of the house. what a terrible time to have a fight! What had started it? Had he picked a fight just so he wouldn't have to be with her for Christmas? She sobbed aloud, then sniffed and rubbed her eyes with the corner of the sheet. How could she survive Christmas all alone and lonely? And what about their special plans for today? How would she spend a long, boring Sunday without Tom?

She jumped out of bed and ran to look out the window. Tom sat in his car without moving. He looked as unhappy as she felt. She grabbed the first thing she found to wrap around herself, ran to the door and pulled it open.

"Tom! I'm sorry! Please, please come back!" Her breath fanned out before her.

He opened the car door and stood beside the car and looked at her. He was tall and thin with light hair and sad hazel eyes. He wore gray sweats and a black hooded sweat shirt. "I don't want to hear any more talk about the people you work with."

Had she talked about them that much? "I promise!"

"No more anger toward Carla Reidel? Not even if I stand up for her."

Madge stiffened. The fight had included her anger at Carla. He knew Carla and he thought she was Ms. Wonderful. "All right, Tom. I just want you to come back. Please. I love you."

He ran to her and pushed her ahead of him into the warm house. "You're going to catch cold, honey."

She wound her arms around him and lifted her face for his kiss.

In Texas, Lisa stopped abruptly in front of the window and looked out at the bleak countryside, brown and dry and ugly. Wind whipped dust around and bent bare trees low. How could she forget wintertime with nothing to do? She should have stayed in Michigan to ski during her Christmas break.

What would her family say if they knew the real reason she was returning to Michigan before Christmas? No matter what they said she would be on the plane tonight at ten. She would be ready bright and early Monday morning.

Amber slipped her feet into her black leather heels, tucked her blouse into her green wool skirt and stared at the phone on the night stand beside Peg's neatly made bed. Dad hadn't answered even though she'd called three times already. Maybe he was off with some girl having a gay old time. Amber flushed and refused to dwell on the thought. She would try one more time before she and Peg left for church.

She heard Peg turn over the cassette tape in the living room and music crashed into the air. Amber walked over to close the door, then stopped dead in her tracks.

Brian Ainslie stood there dressed in a navy blue three-piece suit, light blue shirt and a dull red tie. He looked questioningly at Amber, and she stared at him as if he were a ghost.

"Dad?"

"Hi, Am."

For a fraction of a second she hesistated, then she flung her arms around his waist and hugged him so tightly her arms ached. She felt his arms close around her in a bear hug that she remembered so well. Tears welled up in her eyes and she closed them tightly, then pressed her face into his neck.

"Amber, Amber. My little girl." His voice broke and he cleared his throat. "How I've missed you."

"I've missed you, Dad." She pulled away and tugged her jacket in place. "I can't believe you're here!"

"I couldn't stay away a second longer." He looked down into her face, trying to read her thoughts. "I couldn't let Christmas go by without trying to make things right between us."

"Oh, Dad!" Tears ran down her cheeks as she caught his well-manicured hand to her. "I tried to call you this morning."

"You did?"

She nodded and sniffed. "I'm sorry for what I've done to you."

"No, no! I'm the one to be sorry, Amber. I was

wrong. I broke up our family. Please, please forgive me."

She kissed his hand. "I already have."

He pulled his hand free and stepped back slightly. He took a deep breath. "Maybe you won't when you hear that I'm getting married again."

Pain stabbed her heart, but she kept a smile on her face. "I hope you'll be happy."

He hugged her tightly. "Do you mean it?"

"I mean it. I would rather you went back to Mom, but I must accept what you do with your life. I can't force you to do what I want, and I won't try to."

"Thank you." He brushed a hand across his eyes. "Now, how about if I go to church with you?"

"I'd like that."

"Tell me about the case you're working on now."

She smiled through fresh tears. "It's been so long since you wanted to know about my cases."

"I know, and I'm sorry."

"But you're here now."

"And I want to hear everything."

She caught his arm and led him to the living room where Peg waited with barely surpressed excitement. "All is well, Peg."

"I'm glad." She hugged Amber, then turned to Brian. "Uncle Brian, I am so glad you came. I tried to do what I could to get you two back together."

"Thanks, honey. I don't know what I would do without my favorite niece." He kissed her flushed cheek. "Now, we're going to church and on the way I want to hear what you're both up to."

Peg laughed and rolled her eyes. "I would never believe that I'm involved in a murder mystery, but I am. And it's not a game, Uncle Brian. Amber is actually working at solving one murder and preventing another one."

Brian Ainslie paled. "I don't know if I'll ever get used to the dangerous business you're in, Amber Bethany."

Amber laughed. "Just keep telling yourself that your daughter is a big girl now and can handle herself very well."

"I'll have to try that," he said drily as they walked out the door. Snow danced in the air and fell lazily to the white ground.

Amber slipped into the back seat of Peg's car, leaving the passenger seat free for her dad. "We're looking for Susie Archer."

"It sounds simple put that way," said Peg with a dry chuckle as she started her car.

Amber leaned back with a sigh. It was great to be at peace with Dad and with herself, but she'd be able to enjoy it more if she didn't have a case hanging over her head.

She had to find Susie Archer before Christmas morning if it was the last thing she ever did.

Late Sunday night Lisa let herself into her warm, cheery apartment, looked around to make sure everything was ready, then went to the kitchen to make a cup of hot cocoa. Things would work out just as planned.

Her heart leaped as she heard his key in the lock.

Madge paced her dimly lit kitchen, her breathing ragged. She had promised herself that never again would anyone hurt her. Once again she'd been hurt. He tried to walk out on her today, but came back. They spent the day shopping at the mall, then driving around to see all the decorations that lighted homes and streets. Today had been fun. How could she be sure that he wouldn't stay away the next time? She stopped in the doorway and listened for his gentle snores from the bedroom. Well, it was the last time! Tomorrow he might see her differently.

Jane curled against Don's back and listened to his breathing. She was relaxed and tired after the long day outdoors. Her eyes fluttered closed, then popped open. Don had asked her again today if they could start a family. He was ready and anxious to be a dad. He'd make a wonderful father. Should she say yes? Did she dare bring a baby into a world like this? Was it fair to the child? Jane blinked back tears as she pressed her hand to Don's chest to feel his heartbeat. Maybe she'd be able to give him an answer tomorrow.

Carla lay on her bed and stared up at the ceiling. The light from the street shone softly into her room. She strained her ears to hear Peter, but all was quiet from the other bedroom. Maybe he had fallen asleep.

The house creaked and she jumped. How did she know that Susie Archer wouldn't sneak up on her in the night and shoot her while she slept? Fear pricked her skin and she bit her lip to keep back a frightened cry. Dr. Everett had said that Susie Archer would come Christmas morning. If no one had found her before then. But, if she came, she would be stopped by Amber or by the police. Carla shivered. Why couldn't she believe that she was safe? Would Peter find her in a pool of blood when he awoke?

"Please, God. Please, God, keep me safe." Her voice broke as she flipped to her side, buried her face in her pillow and sobbed.

Amber curled in the corner of Peg's couch and stared at the lighted Christmas tree. Her mind kept flashing to Carla Reidel. She and Peg had stopped in to talk to Carla a few hours ago. Although Carla seemed in good spirits with Peter beside her, Amber knew part of it was show.

"Couldn't you sleep, Amber?" Peg pulled her robe tightly around her and sat on the chair near the couch.

"I did for a few minutes. I woke up thinking about Carla and Susie and everything. I couldn't go back to sleep."

"I'm sorry."

"You've been a great help to me, Peg. You've listened to me all day long as I went over the details of the case."

"Uncle Brian was sweet to listen to us talk on and on about everything. He's probably back in Colorado, or will be soon." She glanced at the decorator wall clock. "It's three A.M., Amber!"

"I know. Go back to bed. I'll be all right alone."

"Are you sure?"

Amber nodded and smiled. "You must realize that I'm used to living close to danger. It is getting to me more than usual this time but I'll handle it. Really. I do have a Heavenly Father who watches over me, you know."

Peg smiled as she pushed herself up. "That's right. You do. He can take care of you much better than I can. Good night. Sleep tight when you get around to it."

Amber laughed and waved. "Good night. Don't let my whirling brain keep you awake."

Susie carefully took the shotgun down, broke it apart and stuck it in the rollbag that she carried gym clothes in when she went to the spa. She was ready to drive to Carla's first thing in the morning. She would be back before he awoke. In just a few short hours all of her years of waiting would be over. Bobby would be avenged; then she could get on with her life. Nothing would stop her.

Chapter 8

Carla sat at the kitchen table with a cup of steaming tea in her icy hands. She studied the delicate blue and yellow flowers on the side of the cup as if she had to memorize every minute detail. The overhead light cast a soft glow over the room. Outdoors it was too dark to see well, but soon the sky would lighten and the streets would fill with last minute shoppers. Maybe she should join them and find something special for Peter. He had given her a ring and she'd bought him after-shave lotion. It didn't seem fair somehow. Absently she sipped her herb tea, then carefully set the bone china cup on its saucer. It rattled and she steadied it as best she could with cold, trembling hands. "One more day," she muttered under her breath. Sudden tears pricked the backs of her eyes. After tomorrow she would either be dead, or be free of the threat of Susie Archer. she groaned and pressed her hand to her stomach.

Could she survive one more day of living on raw nerves? She bit her bottom lip with white, sharp teeth and closed her eyes for a moment.

Maybe she should wake Peter to keep her company. He wouldn't mind waking up. She shook her head and her slender shoulders drooped. She couldn't wake him. He needed his sleep. She glanced at her watch to find that the hand had barely moved.

She'd been awake since five, had taken her shower and dressed in jeans, dark green flowered shirt covered with a warm creamy tan pullover sweater and had finally walked to the kitchen for a cup of tea.

The house creaked and she tensed. A car drove past outdoors, sounding extra loud in the early morning stillness. The refrigerator hummed quietly, then the sound was overpowered by the furnace blowing out warm air.

She rubbed her eyes and yawned. Tonight she knew she wouldn't sleep, waiting for tomorrow to come. She shivered and crossed her arms protectively over her heart. Why hadn't she agreed to let a policewoman take her place? She could have gone to her parents and been safe. "Susie would find me," she whispered hoarsely. "This way it will all be over tomorrow!"

Abruptly she jumped up and walked to the kitchen window to look out on the snow-covered back lawn. Last year she built a snowman just for the fun of it and he stood for almost two weeks without melting away. Would she get the chance to build a snowman this year? She bowed her head and tears slipped down her cheeks.

What if she did die tomorrow morning? What then? Peg was a strong believer in life after death, but she'd never given it too much thought. Maybe she should talk to Peg about it.

Madge moved restlessly in her sleep, then awoke abruptly. Tom lay beside her and she reached out to touch his shoulder, then drew back her hand. It would be better if he stayed asleep. Cautiously she eased out of bed and padded to the kitchen, slipping on her robe as she walked. This was the day. Would she really have the courage to do it? She shivered and bit back an anguished moan.

Jane kissed Don's bare shoulder. How she longed to stay in bed beside him, but she had business to attend to. She looked down at him and love rose in her and almost overwhelmed her. He had come into her life when she desperately needed someone, and had promised to stay forever. "I love you," she mouthed, then she crept from the bedroom to dress in the bathroom. Hopefully he'd sleep until she returned. She smiled a slow secret smile as she pulled on her jeans.

Lisa jumped out of bed and ran to the living room. "This is the day!" She flung her arms wide and twirled around. Texas seemed far, far away today. Her family seemed far, far away. She dropped to the couch and touched her wedding dress, veil and shoes. This morning she would finish the work that she'd planned, and this afternoon she would stand in the church and marry the man she loved so completely. Would he change his mind at the last minute, and leave her standing alone at the altar? They had schemed so carefully to keep it a secret at work so they wouldn't be teased or gossiped about. After Christmas everyone would know. She smiled dreamily.

"I love you, Greg," she whispered.

Peter stopped in the kitchen doorway and watched Carla at the window. Love for her rose up inside him, almost swamping him. He must keep her safe! He couldn't live without her. What would he do if her life was suddenly snuffed out tomorrow? An iron band squeezed his heart and he almost cried aloud in pain. He closed his eyes for a moment to steady himself, then walked up behind Carla and wrapped his arms around her. She felt so right close to his heart that he never wanted to let her go. "Why didn't you wake me?"

She turned her head and smiled at him. "I thought about it, but you needed your sleep. I think it's going to be another long, long day."

"We'll try to make it go quickly."

"How?"

He turned her around and pulled her tight against him. "We could get married today. Run off to a state where there's not a waiting time. Then fly to Hawaii for a honeymoon."

She laughed softly. "That does sound inviting."

His arms tightened around her. "Have you decided to marry me?"

"Oh, Peter, please don't ask me now. Not with tomorrow hanging over my head. Just help me get through today and tomorrow morning and then we'll talk about us."

He nodded. "You're right. But I wish I could help you forget for a while today what's going on."

"You made yesterday endurable, and I know you'll do all you can to help me through today."

He touched his lips to hers, then pulled back before he devoured her. "Did you have breakfast yet?"

"Just tea. I couldn't eat a thing."

"I'd like a cup, and maybe I could tempt you to eat a scrambled egg and a slice of wheat toast."

"Maybe." She pushed a strand of his dark hair in place. It was still damp from his shower.

Peter reluctantly released her and poured himself a cup of tea. He got eggs from the refrigerator and wheat bread from the bread drawer.

Before long the kitchen smelled of eggs and toast. They sat at the table together and ate, talking occasionally about the weather, past Christmases and coming issues of their magazines.

"Did you choose the best fiction yet?" asked Peter as he cleared the table and carried dirty dishes to the sink.

"I have it narrowed down to four stories. I'm sure I'll be able to choose the best one before I go to work Wednesday." She bit her lip. "If I *do* go to work."

He snapped her with a dishtowel. "Stop it! You will."

She nodded. "What about the articles you've been working on?"

"I have a couple at home that I really should have brought with me. I need to do a little work on the bass fishing article and the one on hiking gear." He dried the dishes and set them away in the cupboard as they talked.

"Why don't you go get them? I'll be all right."

"I don't want to leave you alone."

"The policeman is right out there in his car, and Amber will be over soon. I'll be all right. Really."

He hung the towel over the rack. "I suppose I could get them and get right back." He grabbed her close and she squealed in surprise, then laughed. "Will you miss me?"

"I'll be waiting with my nose pressed to the front window!"

He kissed her thoroughly. "See that you are!"

She walked to the door with him and watched him slip on his leather jacket. "Peter, I love you."

He stopped dead. "What did you say?"

She flung her arms around him and smiled up at him. "I love you!"

"I heard you, but I wanted to hear it again. And again. And again!" He kissed her as if he would never let her go and she clung to him and returned his kiss with a passion that surprised her. Finally he pulled away, opened the door, kissed her again as the cold wind blew in, then dashed to his car. She leaned against the door, her hand over her racing heart. Somehow her love for Peter had grown into an all-consuming love that left no room for Mark Yonkers.

She ran to her bedroom and opened her purse to take out the jeweler's box. Dare she slip on his ring? Was she being wise? She smiled and lifted the ring from the box and slowly slipped it on her finger. It sparkled with flashes of colors that delighted her.

"I do love you, Peter Scobey, and I will marry you." She held out the ring again and admired it first at one angle, then another. When he returned she'd tell him that she would marry him whenever he wanted.

Amber shot out of bed, her heart hammering, and looked at Peg's bedside clock. It was seven-fifteen and she'd planned to be up and dressed and on her way to visit Madge and Jane before they left their homes. This was the last day she had to find Susie Archer and she needed the entire day, especially if neither Jane nor Madge had a V-shaped scar on their wrists. She had an uneasy feeling that Lisa would turn out to be the one to bear the scar. She trembled, unable to shake the strange feeling. There was something she was missing, but what? She'd gone over every detail so carefully that she knew everything in living color. What was missing? Maybe nothing. But deep in her heart she knew there was something that she needed to know. But what?

Peg lifted her head and said sleepily, "What's wrong, Amber?"

"I overslept."

Peg glanced at the clock and threw back the covers. "We'd better hurry. We have a lot to do today. We want to find Susie Archer before the day is over so that she won't ruin anyone's Christmas tomorrow."

"I feel uneasy about Lisa. I'm going to call her again."

"This early?" Peg slipped on her robe and tied the belt around her narrow waist, then pushed her blond hair back.

"It's important." Amber carried the phone to her bed and sat on the edge and dialed the number in Texas. After four rings a woman answered. "May I speak to Lisa?"

"There's no one here by that name."

Amber sighed. "Sorry. I mean Elizabeth."

"I'm sorry, but Elizabeth returned to Michigan late last night."

"Thank you. I'll give her a call at her place." Amber hung up and Peg stepped close with wide eyes.

"What? What?"

"Lisa came home last night late." Amber's fingers trembled as she flipped to Lisa's home number. "Isn't that something?" She dialed and Lisa's phone rang and rang, but no one answered.

"Isn't she there?" Amber hung up with a frown. "Or she's not answering."

"I still don't think it's Lisa! How could I be so wrong about someone? I say it's Madge."

"Only because you don't like her."

"You're right about that!"

"I think I'll call that woman in Thornapple, the one who remembers details that Carla's mother told me about." Amber whipped out her pad again and flipped the pages until she found the name and number of the woman in Thornapple. "Sadie Cook is her name."

A woman with a high-pitched voice answered on the first ring.

"Mrs. Cook?"

"Yes. Sadie Cook here. What can I do for you? I don't recognize your voice."

Amber bit back a giggle. "Mrs. Cook, this is Amber Ainslie. Zinnia Reidel gave me your name and number."

"Oh, yes, dear. Zinnia. She told me you might be calling. From Laketown. Carla's living there now. She's fiction editor of *Woman's Life*. Fine girl. Haven't seen her in six months. What is it you want to know? Just ask me. I have this gift, dear, of remembering everything that goes on, and remembering every detail."

"That's wonderful, Mrs. Cook. I'd like you to tell me about Bobby Reidel's death."

"My yes, I can remember that like it happened yesterday. Poor boy. And his sister Susie was such a pathetic thing. Their foster parents didn't do right by them, let me tell you. I told folks often enough that those kids should've been put in with another family. Nobody would take heed."

"I'm sorry to hear that, but tell me about Bobby's death."

"He had a shotgun that someone had given him, a 12-gauge single shot, if I remember right, and I do." She laughed, seeming to enjoy her little joke. "He was in the little hole in the wall that was called his bedroom and he held the gun under his chin and pulled the trigger. Blood everywhere. Susie went crazy and had to be put in an institution. When she loves, she goes all out. She mothered that boy like you don't see much from a sister."

Amber stored that information away to take out and study later. "What time on Christmas morning did he kill himself?"

"Christmas morning? No, dear, not Christmas morning."

Amber froze and her breathing stopped. "What?" Her voice came out in a croak.

"The day before Christmas, dear. Christmas Eve morning at eight. The Brunners were awakened by the shot and rushed in and found him dead. Christmas Eve morning at eight."

Amber slammed down the receiver and scrambled for her clothes. "Peg! Peg! Susie going to kill Carla this morning, not tomorrow!" She pulled on jeans and a sweater and pushed stocking feet into leather boots. "This morning, Peg! I hope we're not too late! We've got to get over there!"

Beads of perspiration dotted Susie's pale face as she carried the rollbag to the car and drove away from the house. It shouldn't take long to finish the job. She frowned. Finish the job? It sounded like she had been assigned a manuscript to type and she had to finish the job. She shivered and wished the car would hurry and warm up enough for her to turn on the heater.

The sky looked gray and dull and not at all the way it should look the day before a beautiful holiday.

She parked around the corner from Carla's and with the rollbag in hand walked through the backyards until she reached Carla's home. She felt as calm as if she'd come to leave a Christmas gift for Carla. Well, in a way that's just what it was.

A few weeks ago she had taken Carla's keys from her purse and had duplicates made of her house key. They jangled in Susie's hand. She pushed the key in the lock and slowly, carefully turned it. She would walk right in just as if she belonged there.

She glanced at her watch and smiled. Soon it would all be over.

Carla heard the key in the lock. She frowned and walked toward the kitchen. Had Peter taken her key to let himself back in? He didn't mention that he'd been in her purse. Had he seen the jeweler's box? She glanced at her finger and her pulse leaped. He'd be glad to see the ring on her finger.

Carla stopped in the kitchen doorway and stared in shock at the woman with the rollbag in her hand. "Jane! What are you doing here? How did you get in?"

"My name is Susie Archer, not Jane Varden." Susie walked forward, a slight smile on her flushed face. "I tried to tell you."

Carla fell back with a strangled cry. "Susie? You can't be Susie!"

"But I am, Carla."

"Don't do it, Jane. Please don't kill me."

"Susie, not Jane. I want you to remember that." Susie deliberately pulled the shotgun out of the bag and locked it together, savoring the terror on Carla's face and in her voice. "Susie, I didn't make Bobby kill himself. You must realize that." Carla couldn't take her eyes off the gun.

Susie clicked a red shell in place. "It won't do you any good to talk about it. You're going to die, Carla. I am going to shoot you in the head just as Bobby shot himself. Your blood will splatter all over your bedroom and you will have no face left just like Bobby."

Carla retched, holding her stomach. "Don't."

Susie laughed and motioned with the gun for Carla to walk ahead of her through the living room and into the bedroom. "At eight o'clock I'm going to blow you away."

Tears streamed down Carla's ashen cheeks and she trembled so badly she could barely walk. What could she do to stop Jane? Or was this only a terrifying nightmare? But she knew by the jab of the barrel against her back that it was real. In the bedroom she caught herself against the bedpost and held on to keep from falling to the floor.

The ringing phone woke Don and he reached for it impatiently, his eyes barely open. "Hello."

"Don Varden?"

"Yes." He raised himself to his elbow.

"This is Police Chief Les Zimmer. Is your wife there?"

Don looked around, then held his hand over the phone and called, "Jane." There was no answer and he frowned. Where was she? "She must have stepped out for a bit. Why do you want her? You asked enough questions when you were here Saturday."

"I tried all day yesterday to get you."

"We were gone until late last night."

"I know. I stopped trying at midnight." He frowned. Why was he wasting his time like that? He had already talked to Madge Eckert and reached her just after she'd swallowed a handful of pills. She yelled at him, and told him that life was not worth living. He sent an ambulance after her. "Never mind trying to find your wife, Mr. Varden. You can help me. I want to know if your wife has a small V-shaped scar on the inside of her left wrist."

Don froze. He'd seen the scar and asked her about it, but she wouldn't talk about it. "I don't know if she does."

"Susie Archer has a scar like I just described. She also would have a 12-gauge shotgun like you have. Is the shotgun still in place?"

Don's stomach tightened. "Is that important? I'm sure it's there." Was it there? What would he do if it wasn't? He broke out in a cold sweat.

"Would you check?"

"Hold on." Don laid the phone on the nightstand

and padded to the living room in his shorts. He looked above the closet fully expecting to see the gun, but it was gone. He roared like a wounded lion and sprang at the closet and clawed at the empty place where the gun had been. He ran to the bedroom and jerked on his jeans and flannel shirt and shoes, picked up his jacket and keys and ran out to his car. Susie's car was gone. His mouth was bone dry as he roared out of the driveway. He had to get to her before she got in more trouble than he could get her out of.

Peg whipped around corners and passed cars even in no-passing zones with Amber in the passenger seat holding on for dear life. She pulled up to the curb and slammed on the brakes. Amber leaped out of the car just as Don stopped his car behind Peg's and jumped out on the run.

"Jane's here. She's Susie Archer," Don said hoarsely. "We must stop her."

Amber stumbled, then caught herself and ran across the yard beside him. "Is she inside with Carla?" Jane Varden was Susie Archer!

"I don't know. I saw her car around the corner and I guess she must be. Honest to God, I didn't know she was Susie Archer, or I would've got her help. Don't do anything to hurt her. Please."

"I won't if I can help it." Amber rang the doorbell and waited. Her gun was in her apartment at home, but she knew karate. She desperately hoped that they could talk Susie out of shooting Carla.

"What's going on here?" asked the police guard, running up to the door.

"Did you see anyone going inside within the last few minutes?" Amber asked over her shoulder as she pressed the bell again.

The policeman looked worried. "No. Did somebody get past me and go inside?"

"I think my wife did," said Don harshly, reaching around Amber to rap on the door with his knuckles.

Amber punched the bell again. "Peter's car is gone. Did Carla go with him?"

The officer shook his head. "Scobey left here alone not more than fifteen minutes ago."

Peg huddled in her coat and silently cried out to God for protection for Carla. Quiet, even-tempered Jane Varden was really Susie Archer!

A car drove past. Wind whipped an eddy of snow across the yard.

Don pounded on the door just as Peter ran up, his face white and his eyes full of fear.

"What happened? Peg? Amber?"

Peg caught his arm. "Susie's inside with Carla."

"No!"

Peg told him all she knew, gripping his arm to keep him from breaking down the door with his shoulder. Maybe Susie stood just on the other side of the door with the shotgun aimed right at whoever rushed inside first.

Les Zimmer screeched to a stop and ran to the crowd on the doorstep, his face red with anger. "Get out all of you! Now! This is police business."

"I'm not leaving," said Don with a firm set to his jaw. "My wife's inside and I'm not going to let you harm her!"

"And I won't leave while Carla's in danger," said Peter with the same firm set to his jaw.

Amber stepped to Les's side. "I think Don can talk Susie out of shooting Carla. Let him try. Please."

Les hesitated and finally agreed. "I'm going to go around back to find a way in if I can." He leaned close to Amber's ear and said, "I'll take her out if I have to, Red. Got it?"

"No! Don't, please. She's a sick woman, not a cold-blooded killer. I talked to her doctor and I know."

Les growled deep in his throat, then finally nodded. "Have it your way, Red Pepper, but if I'm forced to, I'll shoot."

Inside Susie looked frantically toward the sound of the doorbell and the knock, then at Carla who stood clinging to her bed, sobbing with fear. Should she shoot and run? No! She would be caught and Don would learn about her and she couldn't let that happen. She jabbed the end of the barrel into Carla's hip and Carla cried out. "Answer the door, Carla, and send whoever it is away."

Carla shook her head and looked pleadingly at Susie. "It's probably Peter and he won't go away. He'll come in, and I don't want you to shoot him!"

Susie lifted her chin. "I tried to warn him about you, but he wouldn't listen."

"He loves me." Her voice was low and hoarse.

"But you don't care anything about him. Just like with Bobby!" The gun barrel moved and Carla bit back a scream.

"You're wrong, Jane. See?" Carla held up her hand, struggling to hold it steady, and showed off the sparkling diamond. "I love him. I'm going to marry him."

"Answer the door. Now!"

Carla stumbled from the bedroom, across the living room and to the front door in the hallway. Loud voices came from the step just outside the door. Who was with Peter? Maybe Amber and Peg? Beads of perspiration popped out over Carla's face and fear pricked her skin. How could she get away from Susie? How could she keep Susie from shooting Peter or anyone else?

"Open the door," hissed Susie. She heard the

voices and trembled with fear, but steadied herself before Carla noticed.

Carla inched the door open and shouted through the crack. "Go away, all of you. I don't want to see anyone today."

"Jane!" called Don.

Susie gasped and almost dropped the shotgun. "Don? Go home now!" Why was he here? What could she do now? He knew her terrible secret and he would hate her. Tears blurred her vision and she quickly blinked them away. "Go home now, Don!"

"No! I'm coming in right now and we're going to talk!"

"I'll shoot Carla if you move!"

Amber caught at Don's arm, but he rammed against the door and almost fell into the hallway. The others crowded in behind him. Susie grabbed Carla's arm and forced her back, then held the shotgun pointed directly at Carla's heart.

"It's no use, Don. You can't stop me. I've planned this too long. She made my brother shoot himself and she must die."

Don took a step toward her but Amber caught his arm and he stopped. "No, Janie. Don't do this. We'll get help for you so we can be happy again. Remember how happy we've been the last year? I love you and you love me."

"I don't want you to see me shoot her, Don." Susie's voice broke and she struggled against tears. "Go out now. All of you go out!"

"Don't shoot her, Susie," said Amber softly. "You don't need to. You did a lot for Bobby already. It's not necessary to avenge his death. Do you hear me? It's not necessary. You loved Bobby. That was the greatest thing you could do for him. You loved him, and you know that love is the best gift you could give anyone. You know that."

Peter stepped up beside Don. "Jane, I love Carla as much as Don loves you. If you shoot Carla, you'd be hurting me and you'd be hurting Don. Put the gun down and let Carla go."

"Never!" Susie stood with her back to the wall and Amber knew if she stepped out of the hallway she'd be in full view of a window and Les Zimmer's gun.

Don stepped forward. "Jane, I am going to walk between you and Carla. You know you can't shoot fast enough to hit her without hitting me too. Do you want to shoot me?"

Amber eased forward, her eyes darting from Susie to the shotgun. If she kicked out she could hit the tip of the shotgun, and the blast would go through the ceiling instead of into Carla or Don. Amber waited for her chance. The second she saw Susie look at Don and move her finger away from the trigger, Amber kicked, striking the tip of the gun so that it flew from Susie's grasp. Amber leaped forward and caught the gun in mid-air, broke it open and spilled out the red shell. She scooped it up and pocketed it, then turned to see Don cradling Susie close to his heart and Peter and Carla clinging to each other while tears spilled down their faces.

"Oh, Amber," said Peg, her face white. "I have to sit down before I faint."

Amber grinned. "All in a day's work, cousin."

"I like your moves, Red Pepper," said Les, stepping forward. "I had my gun ready just in case."

"I'm glad you didn't have to use it." Amber held the shotgun out to him and he took it with a crooked grin.

Christmas morning Amber sat on the carpet next to the Christmas tree and ripped open a brightly colored gift that her dad had left. Peg sat beside her, watching and urging her on. It was the last gift to open. Wrapping paper lay in crumpled heaps around them and gifts sat piled beside each of them.

"It's a camera," said Amber in awe, holding it up to inspect it. "I love it, Peg! Look at the lenses! I can use this in my business."

Peg leaned back and laughed. "You never forget that you're a detective, do you?"

"Never! I didn't do very well with Lisa or Madge, did I? Lisa was planning to elope with Greg and Madge was going to kill herself."

Peg nodded. "Lisa and Greg are happy, and Madge is in the hospital where she'll get help."

"And everyone lived happily ever after." Amber laughed happily while Peg joined in. "Especially Carla and Peter. They're getting married in a couple of months."

"I'm glad for them. And I'm glad that Dr. Everett was able to come and speak for Susie. Now, she will get the help she needs."

"Maybe she and Don will be able to have a life together some day."

Peg jumped up and stood over Amber with her hands at her slender waist. "And that leaves us, dear cousin. Alone again without husbands or children. I don't know what I'm going to do." She pressed the back of her hand to her forehead and moaned, then swung her hand out and pointed dramatically at Amber. "What about you?"

"Me?" Amber leaped to her feet and flung her arms wide and her head back. Masses of flame-red hair bounced around her shoulders and down her back. "I am going to enjoy today with you, and then I'm going home to see what case is waiting for me to solve."